Sylvan Slough

Chuck Oestreich

From <u>Black Hawk: an autobiography</u>

"A good spirit had care of it, who lived in a cave in the rocks immediately under the place where the fort (Fort Armstong) now stands, and has often been seen by our people. He was white, with large wings like a swan's, but ten times larger. We were particular not to make much noise in that part of the island which he inhabited, for fear of disturbing him. But the noise of the fort has since driven him away, and no doubt a bad spirit has taken his place!"

Disclaimer

Sylvan Slough is a real place – a finger of the Mississippi River caught between Moline and Rock Island, Illinois, and the United States Arsenal Island.

But this book – although set at this real place - is a novel, not an account of historical or contemporary truth. Its truth is caught between evocation and delineation, between what could have been and what was, between *Huck Finn* and *Life on the Mississippi*, as it were.

Don't look here for historical accuracy, for geological truth, or even for cultural progression.

What counts are some imagined people's lives and determinations.

Perhaps we all live, somehow, in a Sylvan Slough.

cover artwork by Sam Luoma, Duluth, Minn.

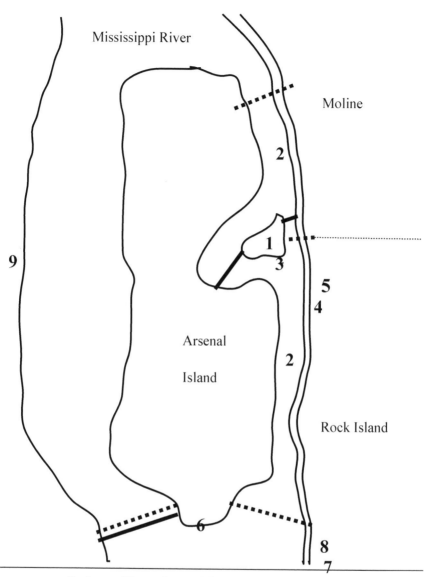

Mississippi River

Moline

2

9

1

3

5

4

Arsenal

2

Island

Rock Island

6

8

7

Sylvan Slough and its surroundings

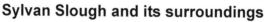

1. Sylvan Island
2. Sylvan Slough
3. The Tip of Sylvan Island
4. The Path
5. The Freight Terminal

6. The Tip of Arsenal Island
7. The Little Park at 20th St.
8. The Pumping Station
9. Davenport, Iowa

■■■■■■■■■ Bridges   ■■■■■ Dams

Prologue

Sylvan – or was it?

It was named Sylvan, this stream of water, this slough. But was it really a bucolic strand of innocence, a place of primeval beauty unspoiled by civilization?

An aura hung over it, this arm of the great river, mashed between a stand of rock and the verdant river plain. It was serene, yet troubled – placid but in flux under the surface.

River willow and cottonwoods eased the stab of water, calming both shorelines, but yet obscuring the truth – and there was much of that – of this out-of-the-way place.

In geologic truth, base weakness of rock gave it birth. The mighty waters roaring down the valley hit a longitudinal ridge of hard rock. The watery might parted at the most obdurate barrier, most going to the north through a cascading torrent of constantly changing rocky rounds, a rapids, if you will. Some of its water also – but limited – flowed to the south, probing for a weakness.

It found one – eventually.

First it surged into a small bay, creating a backwater, a respite from the tumult. But then when the great waters flooded, the swelling of the small bay punched a softer pathway, making a curving westward notch, gauging a half loop channel into the larger mass of mostly rocky land.

This weakness of the land allowed the water to break through and skedaddle downstream, meeting the main flow where the ridge of rock ran out.

The depth of this narrow channel was not great, although deceptive. The river's major water to the north flowing in an otherwise deeply scoured channel fought and bullied its way through the rapid causing rocks. This side-stream water went peacefully with hardly a rill disturbing its placid surface.

But beware. The bed was not even. Its surface belied its depth. Its shoreline was similar – not smoothing beds of flood deposited loam, but groaning of rock punched at random with indentations and weaknesses.

And over it all hung a aura of mystery. Even in its innocent days, its serenity was tempered by something unknowable. Its morning mists lingered longer than the enveloping moisture along the rapids to the north. Its trees and shrubbery encroached perhaps too closely to the water's edge. Its birds – chickadees, great blue herons, clicking gold finches – sometimes inexplicably and improbably flew seemingly bewildered over the water.

But despite its somewhat ominous air, Sylvan Slough was a magnet to all the life that emerged in the countryside around it.

Sylvan Slough celebrated life. Unfortunately, death also rode its current.

Chapter 1

Roger – the Fatal Push

Sitting on an old log overlooking the western edge of Sylvan Island, Roger Pice sometimes was out of himself – hovering in a constantly changing world of past, present – but never the future. He blocked the future out. He didn't even have a concept of what possibly the future meant. Every day was either today or yesterday.

And yesterday was . . . Roger had too many yesterdays. For him yesterdays were everywhere and anywhere. They flowed unevenly through his consciousness and memory. But they invariably started with Troy - Troy floating down the slough face down in the murky water, his shoulder blades through his soaked shirt acting almost like fins keeping him headed inexorably to the Mississippi to the west.

And there was the 11-year-old Roger, sitting on the tip of Sylvan Island trying not to cry. Troy Yelkin was floating away. Troy, his buddy, his best friend. Troy, the best student of Lincoln School, was in the water as lifeless as one of the waterlogged logs which floated aimlessly down the slough to the wider Mississippi to the west.

And what was worse: he Roger Pice was the cause of it.

He had killed his best friend.

Over some dumb arithmetic quiz. That afternoon they got their graded quizzes back from Miss Patty – Ol' Fatty Patty, they called her behind her back. She wasn't really that fat, but the skin on her arms drooped. All the kids laughed at this. Even the girls, when they waited in line for recess to end, wondered why she never wore long-sleeved blouses or dresses.

Miss Patty came down the aisle and dropped the quiz on Roger's desk, saying: "Roger, I think you're really catching on. You got all the answers right except for the last two. You probably ran out of time, didn't you?

All he did was look at her with a slight smirk. But his best friend Troy realized almost as quickly that it wasn't the truth. Troy knew that he, Roger, didn't get all those answers right. He copied every last one of them, or at least most of them – except for the last two, the answers of which Troy covered up when he realized that Roger was copying from him. Troy didn't say anything about it because, after all, Roger was his best friend and had been every since Roger had moved to Rock Island and entered the spacious, old Lincoln School and its sixth grade in the fall of 1982 when he was ten year's old.

Roger came into the school with a somewhat blunt ferocity about him that wasn't a part of Troy's makeup. Roger remembered being somewhat of a bully to some of the lesser-lights in the class, and he lorded it over those younger than him, especially the fifth graders. But that was all right with Troy. He generally went along with Roger's leadership, only occasionally challenging him.

And challenge he did on that fatal afternoon down by the slough.

"You copied me, you big phoney." Troy told Roger as they were trying to retrieve a fishing line with a bobber that had wrapped itself around an old half-rotten, half-floating log.

"Hey, Troy, what's the big deal? Those answers were right there, staring me in the face. Besides I didn't have to change hardly any of the ones I had on my paper."

Then he gave Troy a friendly push, "Anyway, what are you going to do about it?"

Troy retorted: "I'm gonna bust your big ass, that's what I'm gonna do. What if I tell old Fatty Patty on you? You're gonna be in big trouble then, Roger, old buddy."

Roger pushed him again. "You wouldn't dare."

But this push hurt. Troy fell back, almost slipping on the moist ground.

"Hey, come on. Take it easy." he erupted in Roger's face. Then in a moment of pique and biting anger, he gave a real shove to Roger – enough to back him against a small tree root on the edge of the shallow water and trip him, causing him to almost fall backward.

But Roger recovered and, stepping over the root, charged after Troy who ran away along the rock filled shoreline.

Roger caught up with him and made a grab for the back of his shirt pulling him backward. But Troy pushed forward. It was a mad exchange of back and forth movement, a blurring of cause and effect. Then Troy lost it. His left foot hit a slippery boulder and he went reeling backward his arms outspread, helplessly beseeching the air. As if in slow motion, he fell with a double thud. His body hit the coarse gravel on the shoreline, but the back of his head hit squarely on a protruding hunk of rock half submerged in the murky water.

The sound was the sound of something cracking. It filled the humid air and loudly pierced to the whole of Roger's being.

Troy lay half in the water and half out. His upper body stretched, half submerged; but it was his head which caused the nightmare which was to last Roger's entire life.

It was half under water with the face pointing toward the sky. But below the thin surface of the water grew a bubbling swirl of red, making a slow headway into the slough's current.

7

Lifeless, his mouth gaped half open – as if caught in the middle of a boasting taunt. But Troy's eyes – wide open - stared at nothing.

Roger almost screamed, but caught himself before an involuntary low moan slipped out. He rushed through the water and yanked on Troy's Converse clad foot. He was surprised at how heavy Troy was. Then he leaped to the boy's upper body and got a close-up look that froze him into immobility.

No movement, and that strange, ghastly stare into nothingness. Roger reached out with a tentative finger and touched Troy's eyelid. Nothing. He probed the boy's nose. Nothing.

"Oh, my god. He's out cold."

But then he shook Troy by the shoulders and all that happened was a lifeless blurring of movement, a lazy to-and-fro hardly interrupting the sluggish water. Roger sat down in the shallow water, grabbed the top of Troy's body and raised him to a sitting position.

Nothing changed. Troy was a disjointed toy, a slumping body of ragged cloth.

Then Roger noticed the back of Troy's head and a red gash. Matted hair couldn't conceal it. It oozed blood – and something else. Something white and ominous.

With a quick look at Troy's eyes – still staring ahead but now with a clouding opaqueness – Roger let the body fall into the river. It was a body, he knew.

"Oh, Jesus, He's dead. Oh, no, he's dead."

And then it hit him. He had pulled then pushed Troy; he had caused him to fall and hit the rock; he was the cause of his death.

"Oh god, what can I do? He's dead and I'm here. I grabbed him. I did it." He slipped away into an incomprehensible gibberish for a moment. "Oh ga, ga, ga. Oh, no, no, no."

But in a flash the immensity of what had happened welled into his mind.

"I'm a murderer. I killed him."

And he knew he had to get away – from the slough and from the death. But the body of his best friend lay there in front of him. He looked around and saw no one; they hadn't seen anyone when they crossed over to the island earlier that afternoon. No fishermen were on the bank and no one had stopped and looked at them from the back of the factory on the south side of the water.

No one had seen what had happened. So with a quick impulsive movement, Roger grabbed Troy's waterlogged Converse shoes and pushed him into the gray-brown water of the slough. The body floated and Roger pushed it farther out to a point where the two sides of the slough's water – one from the Arsenal dam and one from the power company's dam – joined into each other and created a mild current.

There the body took off – slowly heading west, - face down, half submerged, a plaid shirt and faded blue Levis following a mass of brown hair still erupting with a slow trickle of blood and brain matter.

Roger made a quick survey of the place where the accident had happened. He saw the blood stained rock sticking out of the water. A quick glance located an old bait can discarded by a fisherman. He grabbed it and waded out to the rock and pored and splashed water over the rock until it was clean.

It was the last thing he remembered now that the body was out of his sight. The immutable rock jutting out of the water inscribing its image into the depths of his mind and memory.

And that's what image came to mind now as he sat on the log overlooking the place where it all happened.

Then quickly another image appeared, this one real: out of the corner of his eye the sight of the woman in yellow brought him back to reality.

Chapter 2

Bill – A Crash

Bill went down, tumbled - his body almost leaping over the handlebars, crashing on his side with a rolling thud into the heavy gravel edging of the path. He skidded to a stop, his right shoulder and knee digging into the sharp-sided pebbles and shards. He felt, but could not control, his head being pushed by momentum. He tried to stop it, but couldn't. Time slowed. His head like a ball on the end of a tether defied time and the inevitability of damage.

But it too crashed. His head hitting the gravel on the right front of his helmet, luckily avoiding his face. Also lucky – the impact was absorbed, the helmet's Styrofoam taking the crushing rather than his skull.

In a slight daze he got up and brushed himself up – shook his head and took off his helmet. Yes, a slight concave squishiness showed where it had hit. But the outer covering of thin plastic wasn't cracked.

His shoulder ached and he pulled up his T-shirt sleeve, now dirty and gritty from the gravel, and found that a rash of red was developing, and along with it more of an ache. He rotated the shoulder and no great pain attacked – nothing broken he surmised. The same with his knee, only it was bleeding more profusely. He brushed it off, then searched in his front bag for something to stanch the blood. Finding an old, slightly dirty piece of Kleenex, he used it to wipe away the blood, noticing at the same time that the abrasion wasn't serious – but he would live with a bandage and a scab for awhile.

When he walked to retrieve his bicycle, which lay right in the middle of the path, he felt sharp pain in his knee. But as he moved his leg, the pain retreated and blended into an overall drowsy feeling of slightly shocked stupidity. He picked up his trusty Trek, found that it seemed to be intact – except for the mirror pushed askew – and moved it to the side of the path.

Why had he gone down? His memory had no clue. He thought that the path had been clear, although he really wasn't watching that closely. He was so used to this, his everyday biking route, that he was watching the river and thinking – what had he been thinking of? Was it great blue herons or the lone fisherman in a row boat that was now past him? He knew it wasn't Lila. He had gotten over that – or had he?

Whatever, he had gone down, and now he looked around for some evidence of why. There wasn't much. However, three feet back a stripped tree branch, about an inch or so in diameter pointed out of the rough gravel next to the path. He limped over to it and found that it was mashed at one point; moreover, when he carried it to his bike, he mistakenly dropped it out of his hand and it landed on the path's pavement. It struck him that it blended, like a ripple in the blacktop, becoming almost invisible. No wonder he hadn't noticed it.

But where had it come from? No trees were even close to the spot, this being a portion of the path where the levee was so close to the slough's edge that nothing but scruffy brush and some long grasses struggled for existence.

Just then a bike whizzed by him, not even slowing down an iota. Glancing up to observe the passing cyclist, Bill saw that it was a female; and that she was moving so fast that almost nothing else about her was discernible – except for her distinctively yellow biking jersey and matching yellow bike. His memory clicked: yellow jersey woman, plain yellow jersey. It was she. He wanted to yell. But he did nothing but watch her as she flew by.

She, obviously, had nothing to do with his accident. But a slight question emerged: Why hadn't she stopped? Even slowed down a bit? She had to have seen him, and to have seen him in trouble – bleeding, for Christ's sake.

Bill picked up the stick, broke away the ends on each side of the pressured section, and put it in his front bag. Why? He'd look at it another time, but now he needed to get back home to his first aid kit.

Chapter 3

Edges

We love edges.

Cut yourself accidentally, say your arm or the back of your hand, and after a few days when the scabbing begins, you find yourself, almost unconsciously, probing the edges of the healing. The center is off limits, but around the edges – bingo!

The photographer searches the vast retina-scope in front of his or her eye, and then with the camera puts edges around what matters. And those edges – call it a frame – determines what we call the photographer's vision. We all see whatever the eye takes in – the master sees with edges and makes art.

We have a propensity, almost a love, for edges.

Nothing satisfies so much as the smooth line of a fine piece of furniture. The honed surface of a knife blade. The stylized shaving of a haircut. The circle of the sun cut into a cloud. The taste of Camembert cheese after a sip of Riesling wine. The breaking of temptation with a punch of honesty.

Edges make for contrast, which we love to probe. When black hits white, we head for the edge, seeing satisfaction and action in the demarcation.

So this is in praise of edges – specifically the edge of the cities of Rock Island and Moline, Illinois. And even more specifically, since these cities have two rivers that surround them on three sides, the edge where the Mississippi River meets the two of them. And even more specifically – the recreational path that, for the most part, follows the edge.

But don't think that this is truth. What this story and its segments are about might sound like the real thing, but be wary. An edge has two sides, sometimes cutting, sometimes as malleable and as muddled as a river's muddy edge.

And sometimes as soft and variegated as the wing of a bird.

Similar to what we call history.

Some things that we thought were clear cut – zip, a line around a face in a daguerreotype, for instance – become unclear with time – and thought – and politics – and even sex. Our heroes become villains; the bad guys' clothes start looking white. Truth becomes fiction. And fiction, such as this, becomes truth. The edge changes – both dims and cuts.

Death, of course, is the ultimate edge, our incomprehensible drop from being to nothingness. Its edge is both meaningless and all encompassing - as sharp as a spire puncturing a blue sky, as woeful as ground gravel in an open wound, as shadowy as a bicyclist dipping under a bridge.

And the edge with a mysterious aura in this story is, of course, Sylvan Slough.

Chapter 4

Bill - Never Alone

Beaming into the sun, Bill – now sporting a large band-aid just below his knee – headed east to the end of the Rock Island path, at the seamless junction with the Moline extension. He loved early morning rides especially when the promise of a unique sunrise was in the air, when the atmosphere was puffed with humidity, with tendrils of dark but lightening clouds.

It was the surprise and the promise that he anticipated the most. When would the glowering mist dissipate. Where would the sun appear; and where would he be in relation to that appearance. Bill didn't keep exact track of things like that, but he did usually note where the sun was as he made the turn at the Rock Island – Moline border.

Mornings were special, and he tried to approach them each day on his bike. An early ride was more than a habit; it was almost essential. He usually was on the path by 6:30 a.m. – at least that was his targeted time. And that was true in all seasons, even in mid-winter if the path was ride-able.

His usual habit was to take this early morning ride, then go home, shower, and then ride much more slowly to work, about a four mile trip to downtown Rock Island. He didn't always do the early ride, but when he didn't, he felt something wrong – sometimes his whole day was impinged by the nagging feeling that something wasn't right with his day.

Even in rain, and sometimes even in light snow before the path became too snow clogged for his bike, he greeted the day with movement, exertion, and delight. And he watched for animals and birds, which in the early morning hours were on the move.

When he made the turn into the catch-as-catch-can parking lot/roadway/recreational path jumbled together at the cities' border, the sun struck him in the face. He was almost blinded by its brilliance. But it didn't faze him; he knew the path and the place too well. With a slight breaking, he curved around the perimeter of the lot and then stopped. Taking out a small notebook, he checked his wristwatch and then clicked through the functions of his bike pedometer/computer. Yep, he was on track – seven minutes after seven.

When he looked up, she was just passing him.

Where had she come from? No one had been on the path, in the parking lot, or on the bridge to Sylvan Island.

Had she materialized out of the mottled and misty morning air? He heard no sound of her bike. Nothing except a slight vibrating of the fog as if something large was passing in the air. Perhaps he had been asleep on the wheels, so to speak, so used to his morning routine that he didn't notice her before. But now he did, and she was wearing a plain yellow jersey, no writing on it whatsoever. And her bike was yellow.

Inadvertently, Bill followed just behind her, wondering almost immediately if he should continue or pass her. He hated bikes which followed him closely, even a few hundred feet bothered him. Now, he was about 10 feet from her. Should he say something to her?

He sped up and the words flew out of his mouth without conscious thought.

"Hey, where did you come from? I thought I was alone out here, but I'm not."

All he got was a glance, barely a side look. She seemed intent on the path, and not on the distraction which he represented. She was attractive, Bill noted in a flash, in both face and figure.

He could see that her hair, as much of it that escaped her subdued ruby colored bike helmet, was very dark, almost black. It curled around the edges of the helmet, giving a serrated, almost amusing, look to the helmet. It was as if she had taken a pair of pinking scissors and deliberately cut up its bottom edges.

Bill didn't see much else as his speed took him past her. But he did hear her say behind him in a soft, melodious voice, almost as an afterthought, spoken so low as if spoken to the morning and not meant to be heard by him, "You're never alone."

What to make of that? He was dumbstruck. Should he slow and respond to her? But had the comment even been made for him? No, he thought, I probably startled her as much as she startled me, and the comment just materialized, popped out of her without pre-thought.

So he went on. He did keep his eye on his mirror as he slowly gained ground on her, eventually losing her through the long stretch of path leading to the convention center, called in one of those commercial renaming deals "the I-Wireless Center." It had been built with the name "The Mark," also not the best name but certainly one easy to pinpoint. The place had a commodious parking lot where he usually parked when he drove to his morning bike trip on the trail.

He lost her, but her helmet, hair, and her soft voice remained with him. Was she the same rider who had passed him so quickly when he had gone down? Could be. He had a vague remembrance of yellow jersey and feminine posture. Perhaps he should stop somewhere and wait for her to pass him – to get a closer look at her. No, he met literally hundreds of people on the path, many of them women. Most said hi or just nodded, and that was that. They had their own lives, and he had his. Ships passing in the night – or bikes passing on the path. Same difference.

But, still, he was curious. So when he came out to the east of the electric company's power dam at the head of the slough's cut-off, he veered to the pedestrian path and pulled to a stop. He pulled his bike behind a park bench and waited. If she were riding, she would emerge at the end of a dark and screened section of the path between two thriving businesses.

She never appeared.

After ten minutes, and with breakfast and work calling, he left. Perhaps she had turned around and gone back. But then again, his imagination leaped into place and given the way she had appeared seemingly out of nowhere, maybe she had dematerialized into nothingness, into a figment of his imagination.

He mounted up, and left – prepared to forget her as just another passing of a path user – but an echo kept drumming in his ear: "We're never alone; we're never alone."

Chapter 5

Duane – a dying limb

Duane Holstrom was a dying limb of a living tree – but he didn't know it.

For too many years he had been safe in his cocooned office room on the second floor of the Consolidated Freight terminal on the river side of the vast building that at one time was the International Harvester Farmal Works. Farmal had gone belly-up with the farm depression of the early '90s, but he had retained a job in the down-scaled building – in fact, he had just about the same job that he acquired when his father had introduced him to Big Elmo – actually, Elmo Pasolli – back there in the week after he came back from Viet Nam.

Elmo needed someone who was good with details and he needed that person immediately. Production of tractors was booming and too many were being held up in the storage yards simply because of inefficient trucking allocations. The man who had the job, a crew-cut mercurial man, never returned to work after a Friday night "emergency" that kept him in the office until 9:00 p.m. when he was supposed to be on a bowling date with his soon to be wife. On Monday he didn't call; didn't come in, and couldn't be reached either by phone or when Elmo actually drove over to his listed address and knocked on the door. He wasn't there and, surprisingly, had never lived at the address, according to the T-shirted man who lived next door.

For a week Elmo was going crazy trying to do both his job and also take care of getting trucks lined up for hauling tractors to farm implement dealers. The plant manager, Mr. Casey, was on his back, snorting at him during two different meetings. They needed somebody instantly, too quickly even for the usual route with newspaper advertisements and interviews at the personnel department.

So it was with a quick grab that he hired on Duane after Duane's father, over a quick cup of coffee in the cafeteria, told him that his son, who had been an Army quartermaster clerk in Viet Nam, was looking for work.

Within one week after sitting down in the freight router's soft chair above the wide window looking out over Sylvan Slough, Duane had the job figured out – and, more importantly, the tractors moving out regularly and smoothly – on paper that is.

But within three more weeks they were actually on the road and the storage yards were filled with some actual vacant space – more than had been seen for years. And Elmo had the satisfaction of sitting through three more meeting with Mr. Casey and not hearing one comment about shipping delays. In fact, because he had solved the problem so quickly and nicely, Elmo was looking for a bonus incentive in the future. And it was all due to Duane, the young man, so efficient and crisp, still retaining his military bearing, who could see through the stacks of paperwork on his desk and allocate what was important and what could be piled on the desk next to his, a desk no one was using.

Within a month Duane had the job on automatic pilot. He didn't have to work extra hours, and, in fact, found himself with extra time during his 8-hour day – five days a week stint. He found he could actually stare out the window at times, but since it was basically a jungle of weed trees and discarded junk with only a short section where he could actually see the slough, he restrained himself. He spent more time with a growing collection of magazines about model airplanes and railroad trains that he kept in the middle drawer of his desk, under a folder of old shipping orders.

Duane liked the job, all right, but he soon realized that it didn't present much opportunity. His pay wasn't bad, and he had all the benefits, but with Elmo still relatively young and well liked by the men in the administration wing of the plant, Duane was not entirely happy. He still lived with his parents, but was starting to notice "Apartment for Rent" signs in his below-the-bluff neighborhood in Rock Island. And he was starting to attend the weekend dances over at the Col Ballroom in Davenport, mainly because of a particular girl who appeared almost every week and whom he found fun to dance with.

So early in his work life, Duane was happy, but not completely satisfied. Ambition told him he could do better. He started talking to his contacts in the freight offices around the Illinois-Iowa area about job opportunities, but he found out that his job and his pay was just about at the top for traffic managers in the area.

But then on a bright sunny afternoon, as he was easing back in his swivel chair, taking a break and looking out the window, he saw two boys who seemed to be fighting on the banks of the tip of Sylvan Island. Actually it was more pushing than fighting from Duane's point of view.

But then his coworker Phil Stuart came in with a question about the afternoon shipment to Fort Dodge, and Duane had to look it up.

By the time he had a chance to look out the window again, all he saw was a lifeless boy floating down the slough on his front.

And he didn't do anything.

He just sat there and gazed and didn't even get up or call anyone. He was immobilized; somehow he couldn't act.

And that small event was to be the determining factor for the rest of his life.

Chapter 6

Roger – the big Weigh

And that not so small event was a colossal event in the life of Roger Pice. It drummed in his mind continually, especially here as he occupied the park bench looking over the scene of the death which through all these years he was convinced he had caused. The scene of the crime was to him now both a tattered and blowing remnant of a battered backdrop in a small town opera house and an actual plain of water tipped by a lushly green island. His memory was both crumbling to pieces and as fresh as a bud on a foxtail bush.

Now, sitting erect with his backpack in his lap and his old ten speed Schwinn leaning against the bench, he was back in that fateful Lincoln School classroom of 1983.

He tried to remain back in that confused past, but he couldn't concentrate unless he tried real hard. Sitting at his usual desk with Mrs. Patty in the front and the empty desk of his friend Troy next to him, it was hard not to explode, not to let himself go and tell all.

Even more difficult was when the policemen came in and questioned the class. They even took him into the room next to the principal's office and talked to him separately.

"You were his best friend, weren't you?" said the neatly dressed man with a small mustache that was almost just a line underneath his nose. He had identified himself as detective Rick Friss from the Rock Island Police Force, and said that he wanted to ask just a few questions.

Roger was flustered internally, but he knew enough to just stare at the man without betraying any hint of emotion, feeling – or guilt.

"Yeah, Troy and me, we were good buddies. We played together a lot. I'd go over to his house and he'd come over to mine."

"What kind of games did you play?"

"I don't know. All sorts. But I did get an electric train set for Christmas and he liked to play with that."

"How about outside? Did you play together outside?"

"Oh, sure. We used to hang around after school and play basketball or baseball – sometimes even touch football."

"Did you ever go down to the river?"

"Well, sure, we did." Here Roger could almost feel his face freezing and his throat tightening. "Sometimes we'd do down to . . . um . . . by the bridge. You know, underneath that bridge that goes across to the Arsenal."

The detective reached into his breast pocket and pulled out a small notebook with a pen clipped to it. "I'll be direct. On the day that Troy Yelkin was last seen - let's see, that was a week ago Wednesday – did you go down to the river with him when he went there?"

"No I didn't."

"Why not?"

"Well, I wanted to go home 'cause my front bike tire was always losing air. I wanted to take it apart and see if I could fix it. Troy didn't want to do that." Roger had a story made up that they had a fight about the almost flat tire, but he thought better about even bringing it up. It was too close to the truth, and besides they just might jump on it and ask all kinds of questions. He wasn't sure he could keep the lie and the truth separate and apart.

"So what did you do? The detective asked.

I went home and tried to fix my tire. I had to hurry before my sister got home, 'cause she always picks on me."

"And what did Troy do?"

"I don't really know. I wish I did. Maybe that would help him being found. The last I saw of him he gave a knock to my cap and said he was going down to the river."

"The river, eh? Do you know where?"

"No, I don't. But as I said before, we used to play down around that bridge down there. Maybe he went there."

Roger knew that the bridge was a mile or so away from the tip of Sylvan Island, and it was close to the place where the slough joined the big Mississippi. Above all, he didn't want them taking a close look at the spot where the death happened. Maybe they would find something. Maybe they would find blood on that rock. And maybe they would check around and find someone was in the island's woods that day and would remember that he was there with Troy.

The detective seemed satisfied. "OK, that's enough for today. You try to remember anything that Troy said about after school on that day. He's still missing and we want to find him. His parents are very worried. Are you worried?"

"You bet. He was my best friend and I miss him – I miss him very much."

That wasn't the whole truth. Roger absolutely missed Troy. He missed him for the good times they had had together and even for some of the bad times. But mostly he missed him because of the big weight that his death dumped on him. He didn't know if he could live with it. But right now he didn't want anyone to know just how big that weight was.

Chapter 7

The end of the Slough

the Tip of Arsenal Island

Ancient Americans glided through the looping swirls of water with alacrity, but confidence. No mystery here on the Sylvan Slough side of Arsenal Island where the water joined the Mississippi; no repugnance. It was a place of small waters. Small and shallow. It had no current to scour out depths beneath the fragile waves lightly stirred by the hemmed-in wind. Its water was still, and its adjacent land was the same.

It was a refuge from both the mighty river sweeping from the north and the smaller slough of river water which joined it here, at this place now called the Tip of the Island.

Both waterways slid their excesses here, slowly cutting off from the main current into a tangled mass of vegetation seeped in the vari-colored water of the two streams – dark, mud-clogged water from the large river; clearer, greenish water of the southern Sylvan Slough.

The Tip was not mysterious to those native Americans who lived here with nature; although, to be sure, they did not live exactly right here on the tip. Surer ground was close by where they could build their shelters of wood and bark and skins. But here was good hunting at those times when the waters were down. The water and land mixed so well that man's running and canoeing could many times outdo the deer, beaver, and other wildlife that frequented the place. And fishing was a constant. The mingling waters were a Mecca for the many strands of Mississippi River fish.

This area was hardly large enough to get lost in, so no mystery was attached to it. A man – even a boy - could roam and paddle it and learn it quickly. And even though it changed quickly with the rushing of the waters, it still was easy to adjust to its changes.

But with the expulsion of the native Americans by European settlers the place became seeped in both water and mystery. Stories were told:

A great spirit lived there. It took the form of a giant swan and its nesting place was a cave in the modest limestone cliff above the mingling waters. Black Hawk, an iconic chieftain of the Sauk tribe, wrote in his autobiography: ". . . this was the best island on the Mississippi, and had long been the resort of our young people during the summer. It was our garden . . . A good spirit had care of it, who lived in a cave in the rocks immediately under the place where the fort (Fort Armstrong) now stands, and has often been seen by our people. He was white, with large wings like a swan's, but ten times larger. We were particular not to make much noise in that part of the island which he inhabited, for fear of disturbing him. But the noise of the fort has since driven him away, and no doubt a bad spirit has taken his place!"

Three soldiers were unaccounted for after the 1812 battle of Credit Island, across the Mississippi from Pettifer's Island. One observer from the Iowa shore claimed he saw two of them floating, with horrible gashes in their heads, in the rush of the river on the day after the battle, but it has never been substantiated. Just as unsubstantial are the occasional reports in the past of bodies of soldiers in roughshod uniform seen close to the island. One Jake O'Brian came upon one of these sunken bodies, he claimed in 1847, just below the surface of the water with a Tomahawk sticking in its forehead. When he went back with a boat to retrieve it, it had been replaced with a half-sunken log – or so he claimed from his refuge in Carr's Tavern that night – and for three nights afterward.

In modern times, mystery still engulfs the tip of the island like the fog which on some mornings in mid-summer envelopes the place with wispy feathers of looping silver. Some early morning fishermen claim to have seen women in the water, with mouths still garish red, and mud streaked fancy dresses, supposedly drifted over from the Bucktown whore houses in Davenport across the river. An early morning riser on a boat at the island's tip looking for birds with a powerful telescope reported a completely naked carcass of a bearded man holding on to the wispy branches of a willow tree floating down river.

But the most compelling mystery of this downstream end of this large island in the Mississippi is the story told by four different observers, at four different times in recent years. They, all of them, thought they saw a young boy drifting in one of the island's channels. He was dressed, but with his shirt open and pants seemingly holding him up - and with his face in a horribly convoluted grimace of pain and horror. The back of his head was red.

Such is the mystery of the Tip of the Island – a quasi combination of water and land between two major Mississippi cities – Rock Island and Davenport.

Chapter 8

Bobby Scott

A Lone Roundtree

Bobby Scott sat on the edge of the slough and watched the log floating in front of him. Hardly moving, to Bobby's discerning eye, it seemed stuck on something. Did it have an underwater branch clutching a snag on the river's bottom? Was it actually a log? Could it be something else? No, it was a tree trunk. He could see the knots where the branches had once been.

God, what if he were in the water – just stopped like that? Just a sagging mass floating nowhere? What if he was hardly distinguishable from a waterlogged tree? He heard once, probably in a science class, that a drowned body sinks, but then rises after the decomposition starts. When you rot, you make gasses – smelly gasses. Gasses that make you inflate like one of those Thanksgiving balloons they have during the Festival of Trees parade over in Davenport.

Momentarily he thought of himself tight with internal gasses, floating along the street, held in check by hundreds of ropes anchored by a bunch of kids from his high school. They didn't even notice him straining the ropes above them, so intent were they in watching if the people along the curb were watching them.

A slight grin flitted across his face as he thought of the stink. He'd fart. It'd be like one big, momentous fart exploding downward over all the balloon carriers. Except it wouldn't be a fart like the kinds Jason Brombly let go all the time in Geometry. They were so gross – it's probably all those French fries and chili he eats all the time at Wendy's. Maybe he had weird food at home – things like snails, or potato sausage, or that cheese from Wisconsin that smells like it's rotting.

No, Bobby's stink wouldn't be a fart stink. It would be worse. Like dead animal stink. Like the time he came upon the groundhog belly up on the path. Right in the middle of the path. Dead. Lying there out in the middle of everything.

He thought animals went into holes or caves when they knew they were going to die. This one didn't. He just died right there – right where the path straightens out going to Moline. He skated up close to it and accidentally hit it. What a stink! His nudge showed that its side was open and its guts were hanging out. How did that happen? The animal had been ripped into. It wasn't like he was hit by a bike or something like that. There was a slit right down its side – and the inside was purple and blue and a sickly yellow. And what a smell!

Just then a bike went by above him on the path – a lone guy racing as if he had to get to a toilet or something like that. It's nonsense to go so fast. Not on a path, at least. If he wants to streak like bat shit, he should go out somewhere where there's no people walking or just sitting around doing nothing. He's dangerous, going so fast. Bobby hadn't seen this biker before, maybe he's from Davenport or someplace like that – Iowa, maybe Bettendorf.

Bobby was observant, although passers-by wouldn't think so. With his ragged baggy jeans and his Overdose skateboard he was hardly notable – just a teenager hanging around the path waiting to be alone so he could skate without being observed. Especially since he was alone. A bunch of skaters with their screeching comments stood out. But a lone teenager slouching around the path was nothing memorable.

And Bobby wasn't memorable. Even some of his friends – guys he hung around with would be a better term, since Bobby had no close friends – would be hard put to give a good description of him.

"He's an all-right dude, OK. About average, ya know. Got a little whiskers on his chin and long hair, yea, that's right, his hair is kinda long. But he keeps it neat, not like some of these groats, ya know – all straggly and fuzzy. Generally he's got a cap on. Let's see, I think he wears a Roundtree cap. Don't know what it means, but – yea – that's what he wears. Once I asked him. But to tell you the truth, I don't remember what he said. Roundtree? Weird. That's a funny name to have plastered over a cap.

"Anyway, Bobby, don't say much. And when he does talk, ya gotta really listen. 'Cause he ain't loud or anything like that. He just takes his turn when we're hittin' the rails – follows right in line. And he's pretty good with the board – not great, but he does all right.

"Ya see him at school every once in a while, but he don't hang with skaters that much. Stay's pretty much by himself. Sometimes he's talking with this really thin girl – a freshman, I think. Pretty young – still got braces. But they're not physical, not hanging all over themselves, ya know what I mean? Like in the corner sliding up and down each other. That ain't Bobby. No way.

"Ya, know, I don't even know his last name. We call him Bobby, that's all. Just Bobby."

Bobby – Bobby Scott - didn't mind being by himself. He wasn't embarrassed that he was alone much of the time. In fact, he rather liked it. He liked to come down to the path and do some skateboarding. And in particular he liked to hang out around the 20nd Street turn-out, kind of an observation and rest area just off the path where Rock Island's 20nd Street hit the river. He liked the railings there – and the edges of the concrete benches. Man, you could ride those edges slickly.

But Bobby still wasn't up to doing it that slick. In fact, most of the time he wiped out before he went the whole length.

The guys who came here every once in a while were cool. They didn't harbor any illusions. He liked that – "harbor any illusions" – Mr. Semple said that in Government once and it stuck with Bobby. He wrote it down. Mr. Semple was talking the usual BS about going to college, getting a job, settling down. A bunch of junk. He said high school kids shouldn't "harbor any illusions."

Bobby immediately thought of magic. Yeah, magic and the river – a magic harbor on the river surrounded by steps and railings, and ramps and maybe even some big old caissons where you could spin and flip and go upside down and never come down. Bobby changed the phrase into "harbor of illusions." That's what he wanted.

And in a sense that's what he had right here at 20nd Street: a harbor of illusions. When he was here, he was safe from all of the things that were bad. School headed the list. It was so boring, and so restricting. There just wasn't any freedom. Do this, and do it now. No, you can't do it before . . . after . . . whenever. You have to do it now. And the teachers, just about all of them, always were on the soapbox, spouting this piece or that piece of "things you must do to make your life successful, productive, mature, etc., etc. etc."

They never said anything about "happy."

Bobby thought, "What if all you wanted to do with your life is have fun? Be happy? Not laughing all the time, or anything like that. But simply having fun. Like on a skateboard. Or working a design out on the computer. Or taking care of your hair. Or getting out of the way so other people can have a little bit of fun. Or just talking to someone that you can tell wants to talk to you."

Marie was like that. But she was just a little freshman who sat behind him in computer graphics. She was pretty smart – a freshman in a class with mostly sophomores and juniors, and a few seniors. She was thin – even skinny - and she had these geeky braces, along with hair that was kind of stringy and never seemed to be in place. But it was distinctively black, which set her off from many of the other kids in school.

Bobby was attuned to hair. It was just about the first thing he noticed about a person. He even made up a saying (to himself) about it: hair weighs.

Hair was big, in his opinion. That was why he kept his hair so special. He took care of it. He even used his mother's Pantene every other day when he took his shower. And he spent extra money to go to the lady down the street – Mrs. Foote – for haircuts. Mrs. Foote cuts hair – Bobby always thought that was funny. When his mother took him there once, he found out that she cut his hair just the way he liked it – long almost all the way around, but a little short on the right side. He liked that – being a little off balance. He thought it made him a little distinctive. Even Marie noticed it.

In fact that was how he got to talk to her. One day, out of nowhere, she poked him on the shoulder and said, "Hey, did you know your head's slanted – whoops! I didn't mean to say that. I mean, I didn't mean for it to come out that way. It's not slanted; it's – well, it's not straight. Your hair, I mean."

He turned all the way around and then had to move to see around her computer monitor. Her hair looked as if she tried to curl just the ends and then gave it up when she had to run to catch the car or bus or whatever to get to school on time.

"What? It's not straight. Shoot, my mirror must be crooked. You mean my hair is really slanted?"

"From over here it sure looks like it. But, you know, it's not bad. And, really, I kind of like it. It's different." She put a long, slim finger in a corner of her mouth and started to twirl it around at the edge of her mouth, probably not even realizing what she was doing. He liked that; it was sort of like his hair – something distinctive.

Like his cap - distinctive. Roundtree. He'd never seen anyone with anything similar. Once this big kid, Hopper, who came down to 20nd Street all the time, asked him what it was all about. Bobby was about to make something up, but just then this slick biker woman on a yellow bike came by and Hopper just about went crazy. You would have thought that the woman would be even close to their ages, but she was an old lady, probably as old as their mothers, or something. But she had a nice body, and what Bobby could see of her face, she was cute. But Hopper, he started hopping around like he just sat on a live firecracker. It was funny; everyone laughed. And Hopper forgot all about the question, and Bobby didn't have to make up anything.

The thing about the Roundtree on the cap is that even Bobby didn't know what it meant. It was really kind of stupid – all trees are round, aren't they? – but maybe that's why he liked it. It's something so obvious that it's got some mystery when you try to think about it.

He had bought the cap at a resale place run by some sort of mission located about three blocks away from his 20nd Street hangout. It only cost

27

him half a buck, and when he asked, nobody there knew what it meant or where it came from.

But it was clean and when he put in on his carefully groomed hair, it fit perfectly. Maybe that's why he wore it all the time – it meshed with his hair. And he liked its color – dark blue. He thought it set off his naturally light blonde hair. The blue and yellow Roundtree, that was Bobby.

Chapter 9

A Little Park with a Great View

Rock Island's 20nd Street stops at the highway (IL 92) which parallels the river close to its downtown. A narrow walkway has been cut away from the highway's gutter on the river side, leading across a set of RR rails which haven't been modernized for smooth passage. Hence many bike riders who enter the path here feel they have to dismount.

Then the short walkway travels halfway up the levee where it meets the trail with a sharp ninety degree turn. Again, this is often a dismount for many bikers. The engineers who put this entrance in either hardly ever biked, or just threw the walkway in as an extra when someone said, "You know, we should put some kind of an entrance here." The whole thing is very awkward, especially since the highway which has to be crossed is relatively heavily used, has high traffic speeds for a city street, and has no stop light or sign at this intersection.

The walkway then continues in a slanted passage up to the level of the levee. Here a left turn takes one to a small rest-observation area.

The view from this tiny park is spectacular.

The park offers a key land-based place on the river in the Quad Cities to see the full sweep of the Mississippi passing both a major industrial entity, Arsenal Island, and the area's largest community, Davenport. And the view also includes a truncated look at two bridges, the classic Government Bridge, and its attendant lock and dam, and the art deco Centennial Bridge, which at night sparkles with outlining lights.

In the winter, the tip of Arsenal Island, which now consists of a man-made wooded crescent, harbors a varying number of roosting American bald eagles. An observer at the park can almost always at any time in the winter see eagles either circling, gliding, or the mighty birds at rest on one of the trees on the island tip across about 200 feet of water. They feed mostly on fish stunned or churned up by the river's water as it goes through the dam between Davenport and the island. Binoculars will also occasionally pick up eagles feeding on fish using an ice floe for a dining table. A careful viewer with binoculars can pinpoint the replica of a blockhouse of the old Fort Armstrong. In winter, with the trees denuded, the glasses can even pick up the sandstone serrations right below the replica. But even the best of high powered glasses can not focus on the white swan spirit that made its home there in the past in native American times. Nor can the observer see what spiritual presence replaced it when the fort was built. That would take supernatural powered glasses focused not on the Tip of the Island, but an island just to the east – Sylvan Island.

But the park across from the Tip is a neat little park – unnamed, except for its locational reference, 20th Street. It has been modernized with well tended plants surrounding it and some shiny white metal benches. Besides its sweeping view of the river and the city opposite, it allows for a view of the meeting of the main water of the Mississippi and the sedate water of Sylvan Slough.

Chapter 10

Bill – his previous life

Sometimes, especially on an evening bike ride on the Rock Island Mississippi path, Bill liked to take a break at the little, unnamed park at the foot of 20th Street. In the morning as he went to work, he hardly ever had the time to stop and enjoy the spread-out scene of river, city, and island which lay before him.

It was generally quiet here, except when the skateboarders were plotting their latest extravagant moves. They bothered him, especially when they crashed – went flying through the air landing on any of their protruding body parts and getting up with a flourish of their cap and hair, down turned smile, and quick walk to the side.

The crashes made Bill erupt. Since he was a grown adult with a groomed appearance, he commanded their attention and their reluctant movement to another location.

But the sensation of the crashes remained with Bill. If he sat down and continued his rest, invariably she came back to him.

Lila.

Back in Washington state many years ago.

Lila Shory sprinted ahead of Bill Fleming, the man she had been living with for the last four years, and yelled, "Go to hell, asshole."

Bill let her go. The hell with her. He didn't have to take this crap. She had been bitching all morning – ever since he had loaded their bikes on to the duo rack on back of their two seated little Topaz convertible, and told her to hurry up and get into her biking clothes.

He knew what her problem was. She wanted to go to the "Antiques Alley" festival in Tacoma early – to get there before the hordes grabbed the best bargains, and even worse before they prevented her from getting clear looks at the offerings. They had gone last year in the afternoon and been exhausted and irritable after only an hour. The crowds were vast, pushy, and insatiable.

Bill liked antiques, but didn't care much for the variety that managed to migrate out to the west coast, and even worse, the natural born kind from only a few years back that some enterprising entrepreneurs were trying to revive. The '50s stuff was junk – ugly junk - and that was that! He didn't like it, and in no way was he going to live with it. But Lila liked the unexpected. She loved just to wander through shops and eclectic accumulations. And this festival, advertised throughout the Pacific coast states, was one vast dumping of esoterica. It wasn't a snooty affair held indoors; but a down-home outdoor extravaganza centered on closed off McCarver Street in central Tacoma and branching out from there even to Commencement Bay.

She was willing to get up before seven on a Saturday morning in order to get to it early, but Bill had signed them up for a bike ride, Shelton Challenge, and insisted that they make the 9 a.m. last departure time from Olympia, fully a good 40 miles from Tacoma.

"But, honey, antique shows are a dime a dozen."

"And bike rides aren't?"

"Hey, this is the Challenge. Come on, you've done it and you've loved it."

"Yeah, I know, I know. But what gets my butt is that they had to go and change the date. Now I can't go to the festival. And you like the festival too, even though you won't confess to it."

"Sure, I like miles and miles of tables filled with the same old stuff we've seen in every antique shop in Washington."

She stopped it right there, grabbing the morning's newspaper, her cup of coffee, and a just toasted two-day old bagel. Eating without a word, then still silent, she went through the ritual of preparing for a day on a bike. She didn't protest, but Bill knew she was irate. When she became angry, she clammed up. Lip-locked Lila.

Bill didn't say anything either - except for the blunt instructions about loading the car, and making sure they had everything needed.

She was not the usual loquacious Lila, the bubbling, beautiful woman who he would marry in a drop if she would say so - and if he could get a better job.

Even now as she passed him muttering her almost silent curse, he noted her curved back and taut behind. She, without a doubt, would be the best looking woman on the ride. God, he loved her!

"Come on, honey, get over it. Maybe we can see a little of the show before the ride."

"Yea, sure. Fifteen minutes with the past and a whole day pounding away at the present."

And that was the second last full sentence Bill ever heard her say. The last was , "Go to hell, asshole."

A half hour into the ride she sped ahead, went under a bridge – into the sharp edge of shadow in the blinding sunshine, and that was it. She was killed by a car which veered into her lane - a beat-up Camero with a hung-over driver and a rusted-out steering tie-rod. In reconstructing the accident, officials found that she had almost avoided the car speeding at her from behind. But it had clipped her left handlebar, sending her in a loop to the gritty pavement. The addle-headed driver, thinking he could avoid her, turned into her instead. She died instantly as soon as the car crushed her chest.

Lila, poor beautiful Lila. Dead from massive chest compression.

And Bill, himself on the edge of emotional death, constantly fingered the ragged edge of his own heart and conscience.

He was distraught, deeply. Despite their differences, he had loved her completely. Now, after she was no more, his love could hardly be contained. He was consumed with grief and, as he thought of that fateful day, blame.

Was he responsible for her death? Did she lose her focus due to her pent-up rage at him?

Did he subconsciously provoke her deliberately?

Chapter 11

Bill – His past and his job

Even in the daytime Bill enjoyed the little park at 20th Street. In many ways it was perfect for his lunch break. He could take a short walk on the river path and also enjoy his brown bagged lunch at one of the benches that overlooked the river, Davenport, and the busy bridge and lock and dam across the way.

Sometimes he had to share it with people who insisted on also sharing their thoughts, opinions, and occasionally their either alcoholic or drug habits with him. When that happened, he generally moved along the path towards the downtown until he found a spot to sit and eat. However, no spot for him was better than the little park.

Much of the time when he ate lunch, Bill didn't mind eating alone. After all, he could stay in the mall area of the downtown called The District, a one-block remnant of a longer blocked-off street that at one time was supposed to save commerce in downtown Rock Island. It didn't, but it did lead to many of the unoccupied old dime stores, drug stores, and small department stores being converted into nightclubs, bars, and a few restaurants. The place was lively at night – especially after midnight – but was almost empty during the day.

About the only public activity during the day was a small lunch cart, operated by the appropriately named "hot dog lady," which led to some of the office workers in the area eating and lounging at a space on the mall dedicated to performances, but with many seating places for daytime use.

Bill didn't like to eat his lunch on the mall. For one thing, his baloney or Swiss cheese sandwich brought from home wasn't compatible, he felt, with the spicy sausages proffered by the hotdog lady. But more importantly, most who ate lunch there were from a big office building which fronted the mall. They worked together, for the most part, and consequently had all kinds of in-jokes, and various relationships which Bill could not – and did not want to – decipher.

He did not know the group, even though he recognized a few of them as customers in the bank

Bill was a banker. At least that was what he liked to call himself to himself. He actually was just a step up from a teller. He was an account officer with his own desk, computer, and an open view of almost everything that occurred at the main floor of the First Security Bank of Rock Island, downtown division.

He helped customers with handling transactions more demanding than the simple deposits and withdrawals that the mostly female tellers dealt with behind the ornate customer facility at the west end of the building's main floor. Involved withdrawals, initial requests for personal loans, opening and closing accounts, and other relatively minor matters occupied his time and efforts. He made many decisions and did a good job – he felt – but he knew he was just a middle entity in the bank's personnel structure. He was obliged to bypass anything slightly controversial and send it to one of the three bank officials who made the decisions that counted – business loans, investment financials, fund management intricacies, large personal accounts, and other items that involved much money.

Bill was content – for now. He told himself that he would like to rise to become an officer, and he was confident that if he continued being reliable and non- controversial that there was a good chance that he would work up to one of the top positions. But he wasn't sure that he had the imagination or drive to really succeed. He questioned himself almost daily about that.

He had returned to Rock Island from the west coast in a circuitous route after the death of his live-in girl friend, Lila. First he moved down in the banking ranks to hire on as a teller in Denver, Colorado. That went nowhere, so after saving some money, he found a new bank ready to open in Fairfield, Iowa. They were looking for experienced mid-level bank officers. Bill took some time off, drove to Iowa, and interviewed. He was successful, and soon was smothered in work as the bank tried to make an initial and lasting impression in the booming world of its small community. Alas, all his work and that of all three of his fellow officers didn't pan out. The bank failed.

He was forced to search again for a position and just by luck an e-mail friend from high school clued him in about an opening in the Rock Island bank. Bill didn't hesitate. He had no problems with returning to the town in which he grew up, even though he had no family left living there. He applied and – with the help of this friend – was accepted.

Now three years later, he was nicely settled into his job and his home town. He owned a house on the hill in Rock Island, and felt that there would be openings for his advancement at the bank.

He loved to bike, but he was not a major biker. Although he was a member of the local bike club, he paid his dues mainly to support what efforts it made to make bicycling more successful as an urban transportation venue. He hardly ever went on rides with the club because he found out after a few tries that many of the riders consisted of people obsessed with biking almost as a mania.

When he saw them together, which he sometimes did as they rode by as he was eating his lunch outside, they all appeared as want-to-be clones of this or that famous bike racer. It was almost that they had to put on a uniform every time they even approached a bike. But they seemed to be having fun, and they joked with each other as they rode along, slowly now as they did when they were maneuvering through the riverfront space.

Bill biked to work. For a man who both wanted to bicycle to work and who had to be presentable at work he was in a somewhat estimable position. From his house to work in the morning was either flat or downhill. He found that if he didn't speed up or race, he could even wear his office clothes and not have to change before his 8:00 p.m. work start.

In the afternoon, he had two – actually three – choices. One was to just jump on his bike – parked in an unused room near the back entrance to the bank – and take off. If he became hot while going up the bluff, so be it. He was going home and could take an early shower and don a change of clothes. Another alternative was to change to the t-shirt and bike shorts which he kept in a rear pannier, replacing them with his business clothes.

The third choice was to take the bus. All of the buses in the local transit's area had front bike racks available at no charge to those with bikes. He could get on the bus about a block from the bank, and get off only two blocks from home. Even though he had good rain gear for biking, sometimes he inadvertently left it at home and when it started raining in the afternoon, a bus trip was just the thing.

Bill found that his panniers also helped with the inevitable small errands that he had to do after work. Many days he checked his needed food list, and took off to the Hi-Vee or Aldi grocery store for the items. On Saturdays he usually went to the library, and sometimes even biked out to the south side of town to the mall or the big box stores close to it.

Not only was he proud of all the good things that biking for transportation did for him and – as the press reported – society, but he also enjoyed it just for its own sake.

He was more happy riding through the streets of his city than he was when he had to drive through them.

The little park on 20th Street drew some colorful character around noon. One lady, wrapped in enveloping clothes, had perhaps the worse complexion Bill had ever seen. But she occasionally sat with friends and seemed to be happy with her lot. Another, a nondescript man with a little dog always had a plastic bag full of bread croutons with which to feed the ducks and geese that came flying as soon as he pitched some on the water. Also a few denizens of the waterfront were generally scruffy and unkempt – likely inhabitants of one of the homeless missions near the downtown.

One in particular caught his eye a number of times. His clothes were putrid and his face and hands invariably filthy. What's more he almost always – in midsummer heat or when the wind grew chilly – wore the same dingy pale yellow coat, which he bundled around him.

The singular thing about him was his duplicity and seeming suspicion. For one thing, Bill noticed that the man almost always took a seat on a bench on the edge of the park. Bill could see him constantly move his head from one side to the other, and he looked to be both lifeless and active. He could have been in a daze, but his eyes, when Bill caught them momentarily, gave him away – they were pinpoints of activity – searching, noting, possibly remembering. Who could tell? The man was a contradiction in terms. A sleeping jack-in-the-box or a frantic bobble-head.

Then one day in late spring that same man came into the bank and after a talk with a teller ended up sitting in front of Bill's desk, with some requests.

He wanted to open a saving account and a safe deposit box.

Bill was surprised. Hey, this guy was homeless. What did he need a bank for? And if he had money, where did he git it?

But Bill, ever the cautious employee, handled the situation with aplomb. When Bill asked the man, who identified himself as Francis Balch of El Camelo, California, now living in Rock Island, how much he wanted to put into his bank account, all the man did was reach into his grubby pants pocket and produce a tight wad of exactly five 20-dollar bills. He dropped them on the desk quickly, allowing Bill only a moment to notice the man's grimy hand.

The initial charge for the safe deposit box - $20 – came from the man's other front pants pocket.

The man filled out all of the necessary forms intelligently. He had grown up and lived in California, but now was renting a small apartment in Rock Island while looking for work. A friend in California had told him that Rock Island was a good place to live with excellent chances to find work.

"What kind of work?" Bill discretely asked him.

The answer was a shrug of the man's shoulders.

And that was just about that. Bill gave the man the bank book and the safe deposit key and he took him to the bank vault entrance and showed him the procedure for using his safe deposit box.

After he left, Bill wondered if he should have consulted with Melba, his immediate superior, just because the man physically seemed to be such an epitome of what a homeless person should be. But he had the money, that couldn't be denied. He was a mystery however. Why did he need a bank?

Bill let it go. Probably nothing would become of it.

Chapter 12

The Hawk

The regal hawk surveys his realm.
Mottled dull brown-red, splotches of white intermixed.
Head constantly jerking and turning, complete 360 – almost.
Feathers lightly vibrating in the wind.
Perched wingtail hanging down.
A pompadour, brushed back over the head.
Tail horizontal stripes of black tipped with white.
Impressive, formidable, deadly - talons and beak.
Eyes – black ink dots in rounds of dull yellow.
Only occasional blinks.
Dull white "face" between beak and eyes.
Hurtles and spits – liquid, bones, feathers.
Regurgitating – wide open mouth, outstretched head and neck.
Delicate defecation – clean away from body.
Below the head, one white feather sticking up.
Patient and alert.

In command and knowledgeable,
The Hawk knows the slough.
Or does he?

Chapter 13

Roger – Life on the Run

The man who had just rented a safe deposit box at the First Security Bank in downtown Rock Island was seated again where he was drawn almost magnetically - a river washed log on the shore of the slough overlooking the tip of Sylvan Island. That's where Roger Pice rested. He liked it there; he liked the view. Even though it encompassed the same area as what he saw from the slit in his cave, here he could see the entire scope, could take in the dam building on Arsenal Island, a building which always reminded him of old pictures from history books which he used to read at college or later at the Acorn Institute's library.

He could also see the wide expanse of water in front of him where the two streams of the slough came together after being separated by Sylvan Island. To him, it was a placid pond. It reminded him of what he wanted for his life – calmness, quiet, and peace.

He could also look down the slough to the west and see the stream stretching off into infinity, becoming out of focus in his eyes as it disappeared amid a cluster of buildings and bridges in the distance.

He did avoid looking to his right – to the east – to the tip of Sylvan Island. Looking there caused him to shake.

He also never looked at the shoreline on either side of him, or to the path just above it, or to the line of old factory buildings beyond the path. These caused him anxiety. He did not know why; he just knew that he became agitated when he had to see them and he did not like to be stirred up.

He got in trouble when that happened.

One time when he was on the road, hitchhiking somewhere in the south – maybe it was Texas, he could not remember, and it was not important anyway – he heard some beautiful music coming from a house trailer off near a thicket of trees near the road. He took off his backpack, placed it by a falling-down fence in front of the trailer, and sat down next to it. He listened. It was beautiful, just strains of melody – symphonic – floating through the languid air. Violins, he thought.

All at once the music stopped with a scratch, and a bellowing voice yelled, "No more of that crap. Go out there and catch that bus. You're not skipping school again today." Then there was silence.

But then a noisy yellow school bus pulled up to where Roger rested. Its folding door opened, and the driver rushed out, spouting: "Get! Get outta here, you bum! Missy Atwater is ready to enter, and I want you outta here, hear me?"

Roger told himself to be calm. Just get up and walk away without looking back. Don't say anything. Be calm.

But he couldn't control himself. He started shaking, and couldn't make his legs work, not even enough to stand up. So he remained by the fence, pulsating uncontrollably, while the driver – a hard-looking middle aged lady – looked angrily at him. Then a young girl, not quite a teen-ager, appeared from the trailer.

She noticed him with a glance, and said: "God, what a dweeb. What are you doing, Man? What's your problem?"

All Roger could get out was, "What was it?"

The girl stopped at the step of the bus, "What was that? What did you say?"

Roger mumbled again, "What . . . was . . . it?"

"Oh, you mean the music. You liked that? So do I. It's Wagner. The Siegfreid Idyll. Beautiful, ain't it?"

All Roger could get out was, "I . . . liked . . . it."

The girl got on the bus and it took off. Five minutes later, after Roger had just about composed himself, a cop car pulled up and hauled him off to the local jail. He was there for three days before they carted him out to the desert and let him go. In the meantime he had been beaten into unconsciousness by a drunken ranch hand who thought Roger had a bottle of whiskey that he was concealing.

So Roger tried not to look to either side of him when he sat on the river's shore on a sun baked log across from the tip of Sylvan Island. Agitation stirred in him when it did so.

But he could not help himself now – because he caught the hint of moving yellow coming down the path from the west. He couldn't move his eyes away, although he tried to force himself to look across at the Arsenal's shoreline.

He was locked on the emerging female biker, wearing yellow bike shorts, who was speeding toward him, coming along to his left, streaming along the path right above the shoreline that made Roger so excited.

He did not give up focusing on her.

As he looked, he started to shake.

Chapter 14

Rock Island's western Levee

In 1940 Rock Island finished building an impressive bridge over the Mississippi from its central riverfront to just south of Davenport's downtown. It was christened the Centennial Bridge in honor of Rock Island's founding 100 years before. It's a four lane bridge with pedestrian pathways on both sides, although the down river pathway has been off limits for decades. The bridge has soaring arches of support, outlined at night with a multitude of lights along the arch's edges. River Action, a local private support group for the river and its shore, led the effort to "light the bridge," with one woman, Kathy Wine, heading up the substantial effort.

The Rock Island path goes under it and then continues west for two-thirds of a mile before going under another bridge, this one a railroad bridge with a swing span in its middle to allow for large boats to use the river. But over this length, the path – on top of the levee – runs straight and open. No trees or brush obscure either the river or the city side, but the views in both directions aren't particularly scenic.

Geographically, this section does have one distinction, however. It's the last stretch where "the river runs west." For at its end, the path dips and then turns south, following the river in its normal north – south direction – the direction for the river that is part of America's cultural heritage. Americans know, seemingly from early childhood, that the Mississippi slices our country in two from top to bottom – "east of the Mississippi" and "west of the Mississippi" lodging in our memories like "dawn's early light," peanut butter, and Tinker Toys.

Some of the promotional people in the Quad Cites – the collective name for, no, not four cities, but five cities - in the past had latched onto that phrase, "where the river runs west." It became a motif in self-congratulating ads and brochures attempting to jack up the area's sense of value. You would see it occasionally under a stylized map of the region, prominently featuring the river. Perhaps it made outsiders note that, "Hmm, the Mississippi running west. That's unusual. Maybe I should go out there and see it for myself."

People living in the Quad Cites came to feel smug about it – and slightly prideful. "Wow! This place we have chosen to call home has some real distinction. The river runs west, not south like it does in every other place on the Mississippi."

But more realistic – or somewhat cynical – natives amusingly cringed or even openly smiled when someone used the phrase seriously. Just what is so great about the direction of the river? If it looped around and ran north for awhile, why that might be a subject worthy of note.

As it is, the change of direction from north to south to east to west is hardly noticeable to even a sensitive riverfront observer – unless maneuvering through the area with a compass or a GPS system. The river's shifts and slight changes of course occur constantly and the gradual direction change is caught up in the minutia of varied viewpoints from the river's edge.

Up north at the topmost edge of the Quad Cities, a park on the river at a small town called Rapids City offers the best vantage of the big river's change of direction. It does seem to be shifting to the west to the casual observer, but a tiny island dominated by an impressive house – bringing thoughts of castles in the Rhine or monasteries on island in the northern Italian lakes – commands the consciousness, relegating river direction to a secondary concern.

But the lonely two-thirds of a mile stretch of path atop the levee between the bridges in Rock Island also merits consideration for its very existence. Just why is a levee needed here? For indeed, on the land side of the path below the levee a series of small factories and warehouses, along with the railroad tracks, would hardly seem worth the considerable expense of building the formidable levee.

One of the warehouses is huge – fully nine stories high. But it's defunct – unused and most of its windows broken and open to the weather. The bottom floor is used for storage; semi trucks load and unload occasionally through the day. But the warehouse's business also is rather unpropitious.

Some with eyes on the future have proposed that the building be converted to housing, luring neo-urbanites with old brick walls, secluded surroundings, and – for half of the windows – clear views of "where the river runs west." It could work, but the building's seclusion also is a drawback. In the midst of a small industrial fief, isolated from the amenities that a downtown, especially one that hasn't "come back," offers, it sits almost alone – a nondescript, squat square, barely functional and unappealing. Located closer to Rock Island's mainstream, it might be grist for redevelopment, but other somewhat similar buildings are closer to the vestibule – bride's maids waiting for best men.

Further into the city behind the warehouse, also on the flat river floodplain, are other small warehouses and lightly used, straight walled, and unadorned buildings used by a variety of small businesses, such as mailers, distributors, and parts depositories. They have no access to river shipping, relying strictly on truck transportation.

And they don't even have access to the railroad that is also a part of the scene from the levee path. Owned now by the Iowa Interstate Railroad, which sends much of its traffic across the Crescent Bridge to Davenport, two rail lines still remain heading west and south, occasionally hosting a very local freight train picking up deliveries from the few businesses with access to the lines. The lines follow the river all the way to just east of its junction with the Rock River, and then continue into Milan, servicing another few businesses. Not busy at all – hardly ever disrupting car or truck traffic over its rusting rails – the railroad would not appear to be a major player in the quest for the why of a levee.

Ultimately the answer goes back to the river and its fantastic ability and volume in time of flood. It presents havoc by almost the gentlest of means – slowly seeping and filling any space that presents an opening. With no levee, floodwater would slowly sweep through the vast flat plain of ground created through the eons by many such floods. It would impinge upon residential areas and slowly but surely engulf the downtown, protected on its river side by its own sturdy levee, to be sure, but open to the insidious rise of water from its back or flanks.

That would be unacceptable: hence the levee to the west of the Centennial Bridge.

The levee - not pretty on the town side, and unassuming on the river side – with its mostly unencumbered view of the levee's rock strewn flanks leading to a usually very thin flat juncture with the river – is pure utilitarian.

For path users it's a straight stretch offering clear sight lines and a chance to go faster than normal. Although barren of nature, for the most part, it does offer powerful sunsets in the evening and misty river clouds on the occasional morning when the river seems to be exhaling.

Chapter 15

Jane,
her biking, and her husband

Jane took a break. She had been riding steady, if not fast, for two hours, going from Rock Island to Hampton and back. – a total of about 27 miles. When she came up from under the Arsenal Island railroad bridge, she made a 270 degree turn and stopped at a park bench nearby.

She was sweating and she knew her forehead was red, but not her cheeks. She knew from long experience that when she over-exerted herself, the first physical expression, besides the sweat, was a red forehead. As a teen, she was kidded about it occasionally in gym classes, but since she hardly ever put out any effort during the desultory exercises and perfunctory competitions, it hardly ever arose.

She first remembered it during a game of pom-pom-pull-away a week before her eighth birthday during a suddenly hot mid-spring evening. Gasping and grasping for breath after running back and forth more than ten times across her elementary school's grassy playing field and successfully evading the slowly increasing group of "its" in the middle, she flopped down next to the wire fence.

"Jane, what's the matter, you're red," blustered the big sixth grade girl next to her. "I mean you're not all red – just your . . . forehead. That's weird. Not your cheeks, but your forehead. Why's that?"

"What, what are you talking about? Hey, I'm just out of breath, what's the matter with that?"

"But your forehead's red – and it looks like it's getting redder. Hey, Beth," she called to another sixth grader, "look at little Jane. Is she all right with her forehead like that?"

By the time Beth and a few others standing with her came over to the fence, the redness was decreasing, Jane's face returning to its normal rather pale, almost yellowish, color. She had also regained her breath. Soon she was back in the game, eventually being the third last runner captured – quite a feat for a third grader amid the mostly older kids.

But Jane knew about, and had some trepidation about, this rather singular peculiarity. So did her husband, Fred Tressel – especially during sex. Since

Fred didn't bike, or do hardly any other physical activity for that matter, he didn't see her often in an over-extended physical condition.

But he did see her after sex if they turned the night light on during their activities. However, lately the light had been off – by an almost unconscious mutual agreement. It wasn't too long ago that they had installed the light, and Fred, with a sincere plea in his voice, had said, "My lovely Jane, let's turn that light on. You are so sedately beautiful, I want to see you during our loving."

Fred talked like that, a precise gratuitousness that now more and more irritated Jane. "Come on," she blurted to him the last time they had made love, "get real. Talk like you live here in the twenty-first century with me, and you're not at work, and you're not out to impress some of your associates. You're here with your wife of, let's see fifteen years, for Christ's sake. Just speak plainly – funny, or obscene, or bestial – but don't just mouth the cliches we've heard all our lives."

That shut him up. Like a clam, his mouth clamped tight.

In their heyday, the first five years or so of their marriage, she knew she glowed, perhaps not during sex, but certainly afterward as she lay partially uncovered on her side, tracing her husband's left arm, flank, or buttock with her hand. Fred always lay flat, his eyes – she assumed – staring straight ahead at the completely dark ceiling. She assumed that, and when they eventually did turn the night light on, she confirmed it. It happened the same every time. He rolled off, lay flat, and stared ahead like a startled boxer floored by an unexpected punch.

But once or twice he did look at her, or actually she pulled his face to hers, and he saw her peculiar glowing forehead. It amused him rather than startled him. In fact he even uncharacteristically made up a bastardized little poem about it:

> There once was a girl who had a little red
> Right in the middle of her forehead.
> When she was good, she was very, very good,
> And when she was bad, she was torrid.

He would recite it with a smile, especially if they had let themselves go more than usual, or if she had initiated a new or almost forgotten sexual variation. He hardly ever did that; invention or novelty was not a part of his makeup.

But that was in the past. Now when they did have sex – an awkward and almost ceremonious ritual – the light stayed off and her forehead remained untinted.

And now, on the bench, she was returning to normal. Her skin, though sticky, was not dripping with sweat, and a quick look into her handlebar mirror confirmed that the redness was gone from her forehead.

She causally observed the scene in front of her, but something misty pushed into her mind. Her eyes clouded and shape and sense became blurred.

45

Something was in the river – or over it. Something that pierced her, not with pain but with apprehension.

A thin mist hung over the center of the water. It wasn't completely overpowering; she could see through it. Yet, was something, somehow in its midst?

No, it was nothing – just a log, a branch of a tree, stripped by the roiling river of its weaker out-shoots, except for two short sections jutting from the main.

As the log floated by, she stood up and saw it clearly, the mist cleared. Just another piece of flotsam.

But ingrained in her memory was her first impression: a misty presence, dark and out of focus and below it a torso, ashen and clammy, floating and crying.

"Nonsense," she said to herself, as she approached her bike and prepared to mount it. She checked her watch, and with a mental recrimination about spending too much time just biking, she headed off – and home. She reminded herself that she had worn her yellow jersey two days in a row – she needed to put it in the wash.

Chapter 16

From a park bench

For many years the path ended just to the west of a railroad bridge crossing the slough to Arsenal Island. A park bench marks the spot. Oh, there is a short extension zigging to the southeast and paralleling the railroad track for about a tenth of a mile before ending in a teardrop shaped loop. The early path designers evidently figured that the path would have to leave the river and skirt the railroad yards which blocked the area. They put the loop in atop a dwindling levee, but it had nowhere to go – the rail yards extending all the way to a busy street-highway with no room for a path construction.

So this little stretch behind the park bench is a lonely, little used remnant, a way to see the progressing flora of an urban ditch occasionally soppy with rain water, but mostly a mass of resilient wild plants – cattails, duckweed, march marigold On the other side a wide plain, kept sheared by the nearby Botanical Center which owns it, is also hemmed in by more of the ubiquitous railroad tracks.

From the park bench, looking north, a rather morose, yet subtle, scene meets the eye. Across an expanse of water – not the full Mississippi, but a division of it, Sylvan Slough to be sure - lies Arsenal Island. The view here is of a shoreline crescent of scraggly riverfront trees and, depending upon the water elevation, either a shallow bay or a mud flat. At times this flat teems with masses of geese, ducks, sometimes even migrating pelicans and other birds winging their way down the Mississippi flyway.

On the right of the crescent a wide railroad bridge with two sets of tracks points over to the Arsenal shore, eventually continuing and crossing the main river on the more than one-hundred year old Government Bridge.

To the left is a vehicle bridge access to the Arsenal – and also a way to cross the Mississippi for those willing to chance a few interruptions caused by tow boats pushing their barges through the locks under the massive Government Bridge. This smaller bridge, the Sylvan Slough Bridge, is a two-lane bridge that contains a new addition, invisible from this location – a bike/ped separate bridge attached to the west side.

A history placard is located near the park bench. Erected by River Action, a local non-profit dedicated to improving the Mississippi, it tells the story, with pictures, of the immediate area.

In earlier times it wasn't shoreline – the original shoreline was perhaps 300 yards inland behind the railroad tracks. Here back in the mid-1800s a virtual huge raft of thousands of logs was stored. Floated down the river from the great virgin forests of Wisconsin and Minnesota, the logs were massed here to be turned into lumber for distribution all over the burgeoning United States, especially to the new frontiers of Iowa and areas west.

Why here? Mainly because of the nearby railroad bridge – the first to span the Mississippi. Why on this side of the river and not the Davenport side? Here was a backwater, a slough that eventually became know as Sylvan Slough, an ideal place for storing the logs until they could be treated. Also, of course, the other side, where the main waters of the river flowed, had rapids – major rapids. They were troubling enough for the floating log rafts, but troubling and dangerous for log storage.

So the space where the park bench is located turned into a vast desert of floating logs, most owned by the early lumbering giant, Wyerhouser and Company. In fact, behind the railroad tracks to the south, with a turn of the head, one can still see the last remnants of this vast enterprise – a low, wide building, now called the QCCA Expo Center, but then an important part of the lumber finishing process.

There the logs were converted into lumber. Gigantic saw mills churned the logs day and night, stripping them of bark, slicing them into usable widths and lengths, and stacking the results into bundles convenient for shipping. The process resulted in much waste – vast piles of stripped bark and sawdust had to be dealt with. And the easiest way was to just push them slightly away, and, in the process, fill in the wide slough opening, making valuable shoreline. Untold tons of debris went into the murky water and mud, settling and compacting. Over the years soil accumulated on the waste, a thin veil that appeared to be ordinary land.

But the truth will out. Weight creates pressure, and pressure creates heat, and heat can create combustion. The result – fire down below.

Beginning about the turn of the twentieth century the Rock Island Fire Department was under constant siege by an unremitting underground fire that proved impossible to put out, even to contain. When a burning fissure was extinguished, another sprang up, sometimes half a mile away – but historians surmise, that it was just one fire, sprouting underground through an almost endless series of connections. It was a vast fire which smothered in fits and starts for some twenty years, through all four seasons.

Eventually the fill from excavations and construction in the upland areas of Rock Island was carted to this area, dumped on top of the nascent land, and is now the surface that one sees here. It and time helped to eliminate the fire or fires.

The whole area hedged in by the two bridges and a railroad line running parallel to the river now appears as a cleaned-up urban wasteland. It gives definition to the word "vacant." Over the years various uses for it have been put forth – the latest being an arm of the adjacent Botanical Center, an outdoor garden complementing the indoor displays of the Center.

But history seems to be in the way – that and railroads. A beautiful garden hemmed in by railroad trains? Possible, but still in the incipient stage. Rock Island has had exploratory city commissions try to come up with workable ideas for the area. With the aid of hired consultant plans materialized, but nothing has happened yet.

Here the park bench pushes almost an urgency to mind-wander. Both bleak and beautiful, the eye's scope can jump from a wind swept plain to envisioning history - like a sunken log, smoldering and consuming, and leaving the potential for good as residue.

But the park bench also gives a sense of something missing. Nature, somehow, wouldn't and couldn't allow such a vacuum. Messy and odoriferous perhaps, nature's river land would have life. Man's alteration through the years has brought the opposite – antiseptic bleakness.

Chapter 17

Jane – husband and shoes

Jane geared in, coming to the intersection with the street – 18th Avenue, actually - at Sunset Park in Rock Island. She slowed, but didn't stop. No cars were even close. So like most bikers, she rolled right through before going left on the avenue. Then with an immediate right, and down a slight slope, which with its geometrics always caused her to over-swing, she fought to control her bike. She wondered if the same thing happened to other bikers. She was always glad when she met no other path users here – she would really have to brake hard.

Now, as she rode south to the end of her ride on this Thursday morning, she took her time, allowing herself to cool down. Besides, she always liked this section of the path. Even though it paralleled the park road and was next to a ditch, it gave her a chance to see walkers, boats, a large pond, and vehicles usually going very slowly, enjoying the scenery.

She felt good this morning, in fact with a laugh to herself, grand. As she wheeled into the path's end at the trail head, and swung one leg off her yellow bike, she glanced at herself in her handlebar mirror.

With a thin sheen of sweat but no redness on her forehead, she glowed. It made her look good, she intuitively realized. No raving beauty, but not just plain and ordinary. Black hair, capped and clipped, a coronal topping fluttering in the wisp of wind from the backwater. Compressed in her bicycle helmet, it still peeked with a shiver from the ventilation holes molded into the plastic. Her hair, extraordinary and striking, glowed velvety black, almost luxuriously damp after a summer morning sprint down the path.

She noted that her hair and eyes contrasted sharply with her signature yellow jersey, one of three that she habitually wore.

Her nose rose sharply into a pretty point, she thought, slightly blunted at the end. No classic, just a definable nose, punctuating her dashing eyes.

They were a match with her hair – both dark, almost inky black with igniting depths glowing now and enlarged with the morning light - except when they squinted into the rising sun.

But her mouth was the giveaway. Wide, almost too, with thin lips usually moving and shifting. She knew she was a talker. Words and phrases exploded almost without her knowledge. She apologized, but it did no good.

But she didn't – or wouldn't – while biking. Even on the path – especially on the path she was the soul of brevity.

She was alone this morning, as she usually was on her weekday rides. She knew some women were apprehensive about soloing, especially at a time when the path wasn't busy. But it didn't bother her. She would go where she wanted to go; do what she wanted. Tra la, you know. Life is too short to be worried about every little thing. Besides, she had never heard of any incidents on the path. They probably happened, but she was not aware of them.

She glanced at her watch – 7:43 – and then before lifting the bike to her car's rack ran her bike's computer, a new cordless Cateye, through its numbers. Her average speed, 13.3 mph was a bit low – not up to her usual, but close. The max read 25.5 mph, probably when she was charging through the section just west of the Centennial Bridge. With a clear field ahead, that was where she liked to hustle. As for distance, she had gone 10.2 miles, just about par for her. Her total for the year stood at 643.7, but it wasn't accurate. The computer was new this year, and she had had to adjust it a couple times since she installed it. She could never prevent it from going back to zero when she had to punch a pattern with the two buttons to try to make it accurate.

But she didn't worry. She wasn't a compulsive. She did, however, like to keep an informal tally of how she was doing.

She rode to feel good about herself, as she did now after her ride. But during most rides she also felt good. Even when it was hot and muggy, with her skin sweat-clammy in the wind, she was more relaxed than either at work or at home – especially recently. With that, she thought of Fred, and with irritating vexation what she had promised him she would do today.

He had bought a pair of shoes at Bascome and Barkas in Southpark Mall a few days ago and had been agonizing over them every since he brought them home. He liked them; he didn't. They fit right, if a little tight; they didn't fit – too tight. Last evening while watching the 5:30 news on Channel 6, he must have tried them on 10 times – walking back and forth between their sitting room and the kitchen. But he didn't want to take them back, she could tell.

"Well, why don't you just go back and get a bigger size? Maybe your feet are expending a little? It happens, you know. I had to get a half size bigger about - let's see – three years ago, and that's pretty unusual for women."

"But I like this style. See. Don't you? It's classy but soft and light at the same time. And it's got these new insoles that sort of massage the feet – and don't make them sweaty. At least that's what she told me."

"Well take them back and get a looser size."

"I can't. We checked when I bought them and they didn't have a size – or a half-size - bigger – and she said it would be real difficult to get another pair like it. They were having trouble with this shoe's supplier – Moc-a-Step. That's right, Moc-a-Step, that's the brand. I'd never heard of it before, but she said it was a quality shoe, even if the supplier wasn't very cooperative. She said that her manager was just about to give up on the brand, and that I should buy these while I had the chance."

"So you don't want to go back there and return them and get your money back, is that right? And who's this "she" anyway – some short skirted minx who just graduated from high school - or dropped out maybe?"

"Hey, that's no fair. This young lady – and yes, she was young, or is – was very helpful. She looked all over the place to try to find a shoe that I liked. And she found one. But I'm not sure about the size. You know, it's just a little too tight."

Jane resigned herself to his usual indecision. "Oh, keep them. They'll probably stretch as you wear them. That's what mine do."

"No, I don't really need them. I'll probably find something better – maybe in Chicago when we go there in September. But, hey, will you take them back for me. I just don't feel right – after all the work that she – the salesgirl – put in. And she was such a cheerful sort. . . "

"I'll bet."

But Jane had agreed to return them for the purely practical reason that she was going by the Mall that day to meet with a business client at an outlying office. She could fit it in, whereas Fred would have to make a special trip.

"OK, I have to go out to Thurgood's tomorrow for a 2 o'clock meeting. I suppose I could drop them off. But don't be surprised if I come back with a pair of shoes for myself. Hey, maybe I'll trade."

So that was that. She'd do it later. But she still was irritated by her husband's lack of gumption and decisiveness, something that she found she was noticing more and more through the years with him.

But now she had to get home, shower, grab a bit of breakfast, and get to work. As she walked around her blue Honda Insight, with her keys from her fanny pack in her hand, she almost bumped into a man.

He evidently had been sitting in the car parked one space away from her, and when she headed for her driver's seat, he opened his door and swung out. She didn't recognize him, although she did notice that he was dressed for biking – with black shorts and a jersey.

But she stopped in her tracks when she looked down and saw that he was wearing dress shoes, not biking ones. And his shoes were the exact match to the pair of Moc-a-Steps that her husband was agonizing over last night.

Chapter 18

Roger - his Cave

Roger, now homeless, but drawn inescapably to Rock Island and its Sylvan Slough, wheeled his bike up the embankment, crouching down behind it until he could see that he was alone. In the past, if he sensed that anyone was around, even way off down the path, he either stopped short and froze into statue mode, or he gently reversed himself, letting gravity ease the bike slowly down the incline.

Roger did not want to be seen. He could get into trouble. His hiding place might be discovered, and with it all of his contentment would vanish.

Just like before – when he found a spot up closer to the island and the border between Rock Island and Moline. He thought it was undetectable to almost anyone – be that person on the path, in a boat, or walking along the shore. He didn't worry much about shoreline strollers because it was just too difficult. Oh, in some places along the slough a short beach slanted out of the jumble of thicket at the base of the steep rise to the path, and sometimes the beach was rather pleasant – sandy, with a few rocks or gravel. But these patches were just that – patches. In general the shore of the slough was almost impossible to navigate through. It would be almost impossible to do with regular walking clothes and shoes, but someone in waders could manage it by entering the water to avoid the sharp bushes and trees. But the depth of the water was unpredictable, with quick drop-offs in many places.

So walkers on the shoreline almost never came by. Nobody bothered. After all, the path just up the embankment was paved and accessible.

It was those pesky kids who caused the trouble. Barefoot kids, carrying their sneakers across their shoulders, had discovered his hiding place. He thought he was safe in an opening in a perplexing morass of bush honeysuckle bushes. The opening was just a crack, and it faced and opened obliquely to the shore, not the waters of the slough. Consequently boaters never saw him and never bothered him.

But the kids found his hideout – and they trashed it. He didn't have much in it because he took anything valuable with him every time he left. However, he didn't have much of value – period. He didn't have a sleeping bag, just two blankets that he rolled up each morning in a plastic grocery bag and hid between two rather large rocks adjacent to his enclave.

But the kids found them, unfurled them, and threw them into the river. Luckily an overhanging tree branch about 30 feet away caught one of them – the plaid, woolen one, and he was able to salvage it – to dry it out over a period of three days. He never found the other one. He would have to get another one before the end of summer.

But they also tore up his tent. It wasn't really a tent, just a plastic tarp with cotton line sown in around the edges. And they broke the four branches that he had been using for poles to hold up the tarp when he put it up. Most of the time he didn't use it. But when it rained it was much better sitting under it than sitting impassively through a downpour with the rainwater running through his hair and face. He didn't mind if his clothes got wet. He figured they would actually benefit from the rain – be a little cleaner when they dried out.

The kids had evidently had a pocketknife or some other sharp object because the tent was still there, but in tatters – slashed into strips of frayed green, useless for anything, not even a wrap during a storm.

That was about it. Oh, they had kicked around the rocks he used to cook upon. And the sterno can was nowhere to be seen, probably thrown into the slough. Luckily for Roger, they missed his one cooking utensil, a battered and encrusted 6-inch pot and pot cover. He had left it almost buried under a wild holly bush, thorns projecting from its many leaves. They hadn't gone near it, he figured.

But that was a long time ago – or was it just last week? Roger was never really sure of time. He had no clock or watch. In fact, he rather gloried to himself with that fact. What did time have to do with him? He lived by nature's time, and that was enough. And he kept no calendar. Nature with its varying shifts of sunlight provided him with all the knowledge about the changing seasons that he needed. Through the years, he had become almost animal-like in this regard. He was a creature of the sun, responding to its subtle changes through the year.

Now he lived in his cave – not a brush enclosed hideout like the kids had trashed, but a real cave. And he felt perfectly safe there. After all, he had passed it many times and had never noticed it until he had actually stumbled into it - or more truthfully, his bicycle had fallen into it.

In searching for a new location after the kids had ruined his hideout, he noticed a very slight drainage line – not so much a declination but just a slight parting of the vegetation. He found he could use it to walk and skid from the path surface down to the shoreline where a small but clear beach attracted him.

It turned out to have possibilities – a thicket of young willows grew about six feet from the water. And there was a small space amid the trees that perhaps could accommodate him. But what about his bike? It needed concealment – and close by.

So he went up the embankment again and started pushing the bike down through the rocks and bushes along the drainage line. Unfortunately – or perhaps fortunately – the bike got away from him and plunged down the incline, bouncing along the gravel, ricocheting off large rocks and trees. Then it just disappeared. It was gone.

Roger stopped in his tracks. He sat down and did nothing. It was how he reacted to stress in his life. Do nothing and no trouble arises. Do something and you get in trouble. He had learned that much in his 38 years of life. He closed his eyes and cleared his mind. He thought of water – smooth, untroubled river water, placidly moving through a woods of beech and maple trees.

Eventually he became at peace with himself.

So he had lost his bike. Whatever. In his life he had lost almost everything he had ever called his own. So, big deal. He had lost his bike. Perhaps he would be able to find another. But he had some things roped on to the back of the bike for which he felt a need.

He arose and stumbled down the incline to see if he had really lost it or just couldn't see it. On the shoreline and in the willows, he could find no trace of any bike – or any indication that it had been there. Where had it gone? He sat down on the side of the river, turned around and studied the wooded embankment. Nothing – just the slight drainage line that he had followed down.

Getting hungry, he grappled in his shirt pocket for the scrap of roll he had put there as he was leaving the morning breakfast at the homeless shelter. As he did so, he thought he saw a glint of light, a minute reflection that he hadn't noticed before. It came from a spot about 15 feet downriver from where he had come down the slope. He scrambled over to where he thought he saw it, pushed aside some greenery, and almost bumped into his front tire. But he couldn't see the rest of the bike. It was almost like a vision – a bike tire growing out of . . . what was it? . . . yes, out of rock.

He looked around. He was alone. He retraced his route up the drainage run, pulling himself up at places by grabbing at tree branches. He squirmed himself to his right, pushing aside the unwieldy vegetation. After about ten feet of this he went down too.

Heading into a particular wild thicket, he lost his footing, and found himself skidding, if not falling into a crevasse in the earth. He landed just where his bike did, in a space about 5 feet across where the bank side had opened up, the end of a long opening into the pushed together rocks and soil that made up the embankment. He almost injured himself because he crashed into his bike, but luckily he slid across it and ended upright but startled.

He looked around. Before him the front of his bike disappeared into the surrounding rock and dirt. On either side of him, in varying depths, were water-washed banks surmounted with black encumbrances of thickly overgrown underbrush which reached over his head, effectively creating a narrow cave just wide enough where he fell for him to move around. Behind him the slightly moist dirt surface quickly disappeared into the crack of what looked to be a spring, or some kind of water channel. No water was coming from it, but he instinctively knew that during a rainstorm the place would probably be wet.

However, now it was dry and he was out of sight. The place was just what he was looking for.

But he had to do something about his bike. He wiggled the front tire but nothing gave, partly because he was so cramped he couldn't get the leverage he needed. So he opened the quick release lever and jerked the bike up. It came away freely, and he had enough room to lift it behind himself and then start jockeying the front wheel back and forth, loosening it, eventually pulling it out.

He looked where the tire had been. Through a screen of green leaves he could see the river, glinting in the mid-morning sun. He guessed he was about five feet above the shore level, with a precipitous slope both in front and behind him.

He had fallen into a haven.

What a find! An instant home in a hole in the earth, covered with nature's benefice, and impenetrable to the entire civilization around him. Why, even the pesky kids wouldn't find it.

He did have an immediate problem with his bike though. How could he get it out? He knew he could scramble up the side of what he even now started calling in his thoughts his cave, but could he lift the bike out?

It took much effort, but he did it – and he didn't disturb the vegetation much in the process. And down the bank a bit, closer to the drainage line that he first used, he found an acceptable place to store his bike. A scrabble of young bushes and old tree limbs had just enough flexibility for him to lift them up in a clump and push his bike under them. It wasn't completely covered, but for all the world, it could be taken for a piece of debris from the fallen apart factories in the vicinity.

So now after some time, he didn't know how much, he was pushing his bike up the embankment, keeping a wary eye out for anyone who could observe him. That's when he saw her. At first a yellow patch moving quickly on the periphery of the path, she pumped into view.

He froze, too late to move back down.

But he froze also in both fear and anticipation.

Chapter 19

Sylvan Island

The river is power.

Anything flowing down, propelled by gravity, has force.

That's what attracted early settlers to this niche on the Mississippi River. The bulk of the river charged down the rapids to the north of the island, now called Arsenal Island, following a slight declivity in the bedrock. The inclined river bottom caused both the river to speed up and its depth to lessen, bringing great masses of rock close to the surface and great potential harm to any boats attempting to either go up or down. It was dangerous, but it also was advantageous. If it hadn't been for the rapids, no community would be here – probably.

Boat captains, who could handle the normal flow of the river, were stymied by the rapids. They had either to head for shore, unload their cargoes, and have them hauled around the rapids, or take on a local pilot who knew the rapids intimately. It turned out that both of these were used – and they all caused some stopping, resting, changing things around, etc. – hence a settlement.

And that's how Rock Island and its sister across the river, Davenport, began. It's interesting that the native Americans weren't particularly interested in this spot for a settlement. Down river about three miles, at the place where the Rock River joined the Mississippi, they at one time created one of the largest "cities" in North America – Saukenuk. They had no particular need to stop and set up their village near the rapids, but the confluence downriver offered two streams of pleasant water and bottom land in abundance.

But upriver, adjacent to the rapids, so much water with so much power was impossible for the early settlers to handle. The rapids remained inviolate.

Not so a thin stream of the main river that worked its way, through the years, around the rocky outcroppings to the south of the main river. This stream eventually became permanent as it washed through the higher, but relatively "soft" land deposited by the constant floods. It isolated the rocky acreage, turning it into an island, Arsenal Island. The thin stream – in midsummer more of a marsh than a stream – came to be know as Sylvan Slough.

But this slough was valuable. It was relatively narrow and shallow. Consequently the early European settlers found it fairly easy to dam – and use the temporarily impounded water for power.

The first attempts at this power extraction were primitive. At places where the current pushed water close to the shore, they threw up rocks and debris in 'L' shaped abutments sticking out from the shore, creating slips. The water caught behind these elementary dams gained a few inches of elevation before it forced its way through any weakness in the abutments.

And those few inches had power. If a water wheel could be erected with its paddles in an opening, a constantly turning axle could be coupled to a saw, a press, a stamp, anything needing power without end. And that's what the river delivered.

A number of these jutting out dams, their paddles connected with flopping straps and noisy pulleys to saws – the entire place called a mill - were built at the top of Sylvan Slough. Through a corruption of the French name for mill, the shoreline became know as "Moline," a name which it has to this day.

Sylvan Slough is basically a straight shot for about three miles, except about a third of the way from the eastern end it punches a northward loop into Arsenal Island, forming a soft, triangular shaped peninsula sticking almost into the island. The slough narrows at the tip of this peninsula also – just the site for a more ambitious dam, this one extending to both shores of the flowing water. And that is precisely what happened when the island was taken over by the Federal Government during the Civil War to be used as an arsenal.

The dam backed up about a mile of the slough, turning it essentially into a shallow pond, and this pond with its slight elevation above the normal slough water also had power – or the potential for power. It wasn't long before surveyors looking for sites for more ambitious power dams noticed a possibility. If a channel were to be dug across the base of the peninsula just about where the slough made its turn to the north and a dam erected across this channel, the pond's water had the capacity to work both dams for power. So an early electric power company built a dam – one that is still in use today, although with very limited capacity.

The new channel did produce another island – essentially the peninsula slashed off from the mainland by the channel. With no budding poet to name it, it took the name of the adjacent channel. It became Sylvan Island. Around the turn of the century it was used for various industrial uses, situated as it was close to two power dams. The major use was to melt down used scrap steel into forms and shapes for other uses. And the stone used to build the steel plant and some of the Arsenal buildings was quarried on a portion of the island. When that was given up, an ice company started mining the quarry's frozen water in the winter.

Eventually after all of the industry on the island gave up and left – in most cases leaving much of its infrastructure to rot and crumble - it became literally an urban jungle. It evolved into an overgrown quagmire of third growth trees, poison ivy vines, and non-native shrubs growing haphazardly apace. Some thickets became impossible to penetrate without machetes or power tree-removal equipment.

But a one-lane access bridge remained, although in decrepit condition, and the shoreline, especially to the west, sloped gradually to the water, providing fishermen an attractive place for their sport, if they were willing to endure the absence of creature comforts and the thick jungle behind them.

Kids loved the place. It was a Huck Finn island in the middle of a large community; it had access; and it was close to residential areas, especially a predominately Mexican-American strip a few blocks away from the river. Generations of youngsters grew up part time on the island, creating paths through the thickets, locating vines for swinging, making trails for primitive mountain biking, and generally doing what kids love to do – go off on their own away from adults, playing with fantasy, with imagination, and with their emerging physical abilities. The island was, in a more and more threatening age, basically free of violence, although school boy fights and intimidation, obviously, were present. Kids from out of the area were generally not welcome, but most of them never even knew of it. It was an urban secret – a sweet enclave for those in the know and in the group.

Some of the kids – grown up now, middle aged, some even retired – in recent years have formed a "restore the island" group with considerable success. To a modest degree they have tamed the island, even adding a small welcome center, park benches, fishing platforms, and informational kiosks – along with a drinking fountain. And they have cut through the jungle with walking paths and some single track trails for off-road biking. While still retaining a rugged look and feel, Sylvan Island is a fun place for urbanites looking to walk or bike through enveloping greenery, and get a taste of the industrial history of the place.

Chapter 20

Duane – His Job

Duane Holstrom ruled the path. Nobody knew him, saw him, or cared about him, but he ruled. From his creaky desk chair at Consolidated Freight, he was master. He knew all.

He was omnipotent, but impotent – well, maybe not quite.

He sat at his desk and like his winter friends, the bald eagles, he saw everything, especially on the Sylvan Slough path. He was attuned to movement. Let anything move on the path and it was within his ken. He noted it, and dealt with it.

And what was best from his point of view was that nobody knew he was looking at them. He was just about invisible – a phantom of the path, that was Duane Holstrom.

Duane had the best shift of the two shift job. And that was all right with him. It left him quantities of time to do what he really loved to do: watch. And he had the best work time to do it – from noon to 8 p.m. every day, five days a week. Sometimes he had to work weekends, but he always had what he and Wilber, his fellow traffic manager, called the afternoon shift. He had the seniority.

Wilber didn't have such a neat set-up. Wilber had the four to noon. The freight company split the shifts at noon, so that one man wouldn't have an all day shift when the truck traffic in and out was heaviest. They thought that would take too much concentration. Well, they were wrong about that, and Duane and Wilber did nothing to disabuse them of the truth of the job.

For Duane, after his years on the job, the most concentration needed was simply to stay alert, to not fall asleep. Quite frankly there was simply not much to do – and unfortunately the pay reflected that. But in his 35 years at this traffic manager's job, Duane made enough to decently support himself. It would be different if he were married and had kids. Actually, married wouldn't be so bad, since he assumed that his wife would also have a job. But raising kids on his salary would be almost impossible. Duane didn't own a home – he had been renting the same three room apartment for some twenty years now, in the old section of Rock Island, an area some of the residents called by an early name, Broadway, after one of the early churches in the area. He felt that he owned it. It was his, despite what his landlord, old Mrs. Beatty, had to say about it.

Duane both liked and disliked what he did: lining up the outgoing products with the ingoing trucks. It certainly wasn't demanding, and it was isolated, which he liked because he was not much for social gatherings and things like that. He could get along with people all right, but he was naturally shy – always had been.

But the job was boring. That was why he had bought the binoculars some 15 years ago. It was a mini-binocular, which he carried in his lunch pail every day. He took it with him every evening when his shift ended. He didn't want anyone to know he spent a good part of his time watching the slough through his window. Also he didn't want it to get around that his eyes were getting bad. That would not be acceptable.

He was happy with the afternoon and evening shift. The truckers kept him fairly busy – enough to keep him officially occupied. But the slough path also was busy. Just when his job responsibilities started to ease off and he had to polish off his reports for the day, around 6 p.m., the path usage picked up. People took a walk or a bike ride after work or in the early evening before the sun went down. And many just came down to the slough to watch the sunset.

The section of the path opposite his office was a particularly nice place to watch the effect of the setting sun. Although the big Arsenal Island and its screen of trees eliminated a direct view of the sun, its light filtered through creating subtle colors on the usually placid water. Sometimes spectacular cloud formations also colored the sky-scape.

And sometimes off to his right, hovering over Sylvan Island, Duane could discern a faint glow of evanescent, misty air, usually a dull gray or murky brown. It appeared haphazardly with no connection to the prevailing weather conditions. It was just there – occasionally.

Duane always noted this. If fact he had a little dollar-store notebook, sort of a diary, where he wrote down anything exceptional that he saw on his watch. He tried to note when the mist appeared.

And he also noted other things. One thing that was filling up the little book right now was miss yellow jersey, or as he called her: My Yellow Bird.

Chapter 21

The Path

Between a path entrance close to downtown Rock Island and the Rock Island/Moline border at Sylvan Island is a distance of 1.5 miles. The path runs for this distance with no other access or departure points. And, not like most paths, it's literally impossible to leave or enter through unofficial footpaths or openings in the brush or woods.

A sturdy chain-link fence walls off the path on the land side for almost all of its length. And on the river side is a steep drop-off down to the level of the river, or more technically, the Sylvan Slough. The drop-off is about 15 feet high, and it effectively acts as a levee, although it doesn't have the mounded look of most Mississippi levees.

This was and is industrial land – the site, most prominently, of the world famous International Harvester Farmal Tractor factory for a good fifty years. Now that the company is no longer in existence, the rambling building – one of the largest free standing buildings in the world – hosts a number of uses – from warehousing, to light manufacturing, to industrial baking. And just to the west of the massive building a regional railroad commands a multi-tracked switching operation. A few of the out buildings surrounding the old tractor factory have been allowed to fall into ruin, some of them picturesque montages of broken windows, leaning smokestacks, and rusting girders. But they all have been fenced off from the path.

Much of the path is the riverside 15-foot edge of a roadway which served the factory area in the past. The chain-link fence supports have been drilled into the blacktopped surface, and the fence runs, with no opening, like a shot, along side the path. And the foundation of this roadway, pushed into place as the area was gradually leveled back in the 19th Century, and consisting of a mixture of rock, soil, clay and castoffs from the factories, forms the basis of the levee now. It is settled and stable.

In many ways the path here is a triumph. Often when industry or commercial interests touch waterfronts the shorelines are inviolate – completely out-of-bounds for the general public. Any path must make a looping detour around the long standing property. Not so here. The path making incentives of the 1990s, combined with the decline of the prominent rust belt industrial giant, International Harvester, allowed the public to gain control of this unique river edge opportunity. Now the path is a quiet retreat, surrounded on one side by emerging commerce, and the other side by the slough and the massive Arsenal Island with its heavy industrial uses.

And the path designers did the best that the space allowed.

It's certainly not a pretty path, threading its way as it does through the debris of more than a hundred years of industrial might. The path is at the backside of what was the tractor factory, and as such it was never a pretty sight. Actually all along adjacent to the roadway - which was strictly a shipping facility, not a thoroughfare – the land became a temporary, sometimes permanent, dump.

One distraction for some is the lack of outlets. And when this is combined with the generally disreputable view on the other side of the chain-link fence and the rough foliage on the embankment to the slough, some path users feel a heightened sense of anxiety. How could I get help if something happened to me here? Could I be attacked here? There are no exits, no places from which to escape; I'll be trapped.

The path here is also, perhaps for the reason above, underused. Traffic is not heavy – with only occasional bikers and joggers. Very few people on foot enjoy this portion, except for the fishermen on the shoreline close to the eastern entrance in Moline. A path user can usually count on privacy through most of the passage.

However, this heightened anxiety is somewhat unfounded. Throughout its entire history no one has been attacked, robbed, mugged, or assaulted on the entire path, much less this section. It's very isolation prevents perpetrators from effective operation. They would have to wait inordinate amounts of time for the proper victim to appear. And since there is literally no way out, they could be easily apprehended at either of the exits. Moreover, many workers at the businesses just on the other side of the chain-link fence are constantly working near the path. Any attack would most assuredly be heard and, if not thwarted, at least the police would be alerted and the perpetrator apprehended at one of the exits. It's almost a given in modern times that path users have cell phones ready to give an alert.

Through most of the year the path is confined between the chain-link fence on one side and the almost impenetrable scrub foliage of the embankment on the other. In the winter, however, when the path isn't snowed in, and the foliage's leaves have fallen, the path presents a unimpaired view of the slough and Arsenal Island on the other side.

It's not a beautiful sight; but distinctive and sometimes memorable.

Chapter 22

Bill – dating Rosie

"Damn," Bill thought, "What am I wearing these shoes for?"

Bill was in a scramble this morning. Running late, it wasn't until he had biked into the path entrance in downtown Rock Island that he noticed he wasn't wearing his usual biking shoes. He was wearing the shoes he had been wearing off and on to the office ever since he bought them about a month before

"Damn, my morning is really screwed up and now I've got these on."

Bill had ignored his alarm clock – had punched it and then slipped back off to sleep – because he had been out last night and had a few beers too many. Actually it wasn't the beer so much as it was Rosie – Rose Callahan, who worked two buildings away from him at the Plaza Office Building in downtown Rock Island. Her office dealt with importing parts for machine shops, and she was second in the company, answering only to the owner and manager, Seth Barkis.

Bill had been badgering her for weeks before last night to go out with him. He met her occasionally during lunch when the weather was amenable on the outdoor stage down the plaza from their office buildings. She was in the habit of buying a sandwich and a cola from Vera, the "hot dog lady," a lunch vender who brought in her sausage wagon every work day all the way from East Moline, ten miles away. Bill invariably had his brown bagged sandwich.

The "lady" was a character – customers couldn't buy a sausage without having her slather it with her Hootie's mustard, a product made locally – "out of old tires dug up from the riverbank" - Bill told her one day as she squirted some on a Chicago style Vienna hotdog, which he bought when he forgot his regular lunch. "The only reason you put this stuff on is so we buy more of your drinks. If you don't cool it with a can of Pepsi, your throat would be eaten right away, right, Vera?" Vera pointed the plastic container of mustard at his belt, and said, "Watch out, banker boy, or I'll press this and something else will be eaten right away."

Rosie hooted when she heard it.

Rosie was almost as much of a hoot as Vera. But Rosie – about Bill's age and attractive in a soft sort of way – also had a way of disarming Bill – or almost every man she came in contact with – with a chin-up, disconcerting air. "I don't need you," her cleft chin proclaimed. And then after a staid pause, she would squint and pucker her mouth, and say something like, "in my bedroom in the morning." Invariably when she shifted into banter like that, she would grab the closest part of the clothing of the person she was talking to – a sleeve, or a pants leg. One time when Bill was sitting on the floor of the stage cross-legged in a group of fellow lunch eaters, she had grabbed his sock and massaged it so hard he had to pull away in pain.

"Boy, cut it out! You really know how to sock it to someone," Bill yipped.

"Number one, I'm not a boy. And number two, if anyone is going to sock anyone, I want pure fine-combed cotton, not that flimsy polyester covering you have under your new shoes. Hey, everyone, look at Bill's shoes. Pretty classy. Turn your foot, Bill, let's have a look. Hey, Moc-a-Steps. I'm impressed.

"Yeah, they're pretty neat – and inexpensive. They had a midnight sale at the American Indian – ah, native American – wigwam up in Tomahawk, Wisconsin, when I was up there on a canoe trip recently."

Rosie couldn't be bluffed: "Bury it Bill. Bury the hatchet." Everyone laughed, and as a convenient exit, busy Miss Callahan got up and brushed herself off with a, "I have to bury the crooked books this afternoon. I don't know what he does with my accounts, but I am going to be buried in work if I don't get back right now. See you all next time."

Then yesterday, as they walked back to their respective buildings, Bill once again asked Rosie for a date. "Have you seen the latest TAS film at the Brew and View yet?"

A TAS film, they all agreed was what the small, independent theater served along with a local microbrew and the ubiquitous Budweiser – TAS standing for "Talking About Sex."

"You mean, 'The Whole American?' No, I haven't. How about you?"

"Nope. Then it's a deal. I'll pick up at, let's see – a work night – how about the early showing – 7 o'clock?" Bill did not have any hopes that she would accept his invitation. She had declined many times in the past, but she was so friendly – and attractive to him – that he kept at it.

"OK, at seven. I'll be watching. Don't bother to ring the bell; it's too complicated to get in. And besides my neighbors might want to know who the handsome guy ringing my doorbell is – and I'll have to tell them that he's my new Sears delivery man, or my accountant, or my new live-in lover."

"Rosie, what did you have for lunch? What did Vera put on your brat besides the Hootie's mustard? Not only handsome, but live-in lover. I can't believe it."

The movie was good – both thoughtful and sensuous. The Black and Tan they both had at O'Mally's Irish Bar afterwords was satisfying. Less than satisfactory was Rosie's somewhat brusque goodbye at her door – no touching, no kiss, for heaven's sake, and no invitation to come in. Just a pleasant, "Thanks, Bill. In spite of it all, I did have a good time. You're a neat guy and I like you. Who knows, I might even see you again – like tomorrow lunch time on the stage."

Bill had gone back to O'Mally's where he met three old friends from high school. They all spent too much time – and too many of the frothy Guinness stouts – catching up with both old times and the present. In the restroom Bill glanced as this watch, noticed it was five to one, and scooted. He had enough sense for that, and to take it very easy on the drive home – which wasn't far, only a couple of miles.

And now – with a slight headache and a realization that he was going to be late for work, he was heading for work through a parking lot wearing his Mock-a-Steps with his mouth open trying to think of what to say to her – the woman in yellow who was just now putting her bike on the carrier attached to her snazzy little car.

All he could think of was: "Stupid! Putting on these crazy office shoes. Ridiculous."

By the time he started to blurt out a greeting to her, she was in her car staring intently ahead as she maneuvered out of her space in the parking lot.

Chapter 23

Roger - Bones and Coins

Roger Pice knew he had to take another trip. His funds were running low and it was getting to be time to replenish them. He'd need to take another trip to the bank downtown.

As he thought of the process of getting into the bank's vault with its many locked drawers for safe deposit customers, it came back to him again.

Coins. Gold coins. Old gold coins.

How long ago was it? A couple years, probably, but he couldn't be precise.

But he did remember that he was miserable, living along the banks of the slough in his dank cave with his bike nearby and usually some river animals scurrying around in the middle of the night.

And then the rain came. One day, two days . . . it never let up and he had to drag himself out to go to the rescue mission just to get some food, a meal to last him a day.

Then the water started to rise. It edged around the entrance to his cave, through the bushes that screened it from the water and the path. He stared at it, but could do nothing.

And the rain kept coming. Sometimes in downpours; sometimes in driblets. But it never really stopped.

Soon it was on the floor of his cave, seeping seemingly up from the ground, slowly, incrementally, and insidiously. He had to take his blanket and drape it on a tree limb on one side of the cave. And he couldn't sit; he had to stand, and even then his shoes became wetter and wetter.

He debated whether to move, to leave his cave for a dryer place, maybe even the mission shelter. But no, he couldn't do that. He was terrified of that, but he wasn't sure why. Even the thought of sleeping, living, some place in public around here, sent him in a frenzy of panic. No . . . no . . . no!

Then it broke. Somewhere something gave way. Somewhere up river a barrier gave way and water gushed through, tearing through the opening - and rising.

Rain swelled. Rushing water inundated the slough in a manner of minutes, it seemed to him. He had to crawl into the tree branches around him and watch his few possessions – a Sterno stove, a water bottle, his blackened iron pan, a few extra items of clothing - all either go under the roiling water or float to the black back of the cave.

Then with a roar and intense velocity, a great wave of rusty water rushed through the cave, hit the earth in its back and reverberated, came rushing back at him, hanging as he was from the side of this cave.

But that was that. It stopped, almost as suddenly as it began. The water gurgled as it receded. It was as if somewhere a giant plug had been pulled, or a plumber's helper had finally opened a prodigious drain.

In a matter of minutes Roger was able to put his feet on the now muddy floor of his cave. Surprisingly the mud wasn't that deep, the river hadn't had time to deposit much of its residue.

But something was wrong. Something was different.

His cave wasn't the same. It was altered. Somehow it seemed bigger, more open.

And deeper.

Roger stood, leaning against the side of the cave, afraid to sit on the thinly muddy surface where he usually sat in the cross-legged position that he had come to think was normal. He was turned about and out of his element. Something was definable different and he was afraid to even attempt to find out.

He stood for hours. He was still standing when, like the eastern dawn on a cloudy day, increments of light suffused through his leafy cave. Roger hardly noticed it. He stared ahead, not bothered so much by what the flood had done to his immediate surroundings, but something gnawing in his chest – some apprehension of change that was palpable and near.

Outside clouds scuttled in a brisk wind, which tattered them into wisps of web, tendrils of gray threads. But they brought light – for the first time in days. The light poked into the cave and shook the somnolent Roger into a dazed consciousness.

He looked around – seemingly for the first time in days. Nothing much had changed. Still the vegetated walls of the cave were intact, now moving excitedly in the brisk wind which occasionally swept into the cave in gusts. He slowly turned his head and surveyed the dank space where he had been living during these depressing months of summer.

But something was changed. Not just mud on the surface of the cave or the residue of his primitive household goods. No, something loomed in the back of the cave – in the area where it penetrated the dank wall of the dirt embankment that sloped up to the levee.

Something had shifted. Something was there that hadn't been there before. A vortex, a cavity, an enlargement – many vague shapes slowly filtered into Roger's mind. But he couldn't tell for sure. In the murky light of the storm's aftermath he could not make out what the difference was.

As he stared into the nether regions of the back of the cave, as if in some undefined answer, the storm clouds, reduced now to wispy fragments, scuttled away and pure, yellow sunshine cut into Roger's consciousness.

Although dappled by the greenery around the walls of the cave, the light nevertheless opened up what had been darkness into some semblance of dappled light.

Roger stared and slowly made out a vague small shape – perhaps an irregular branch of a tree or large shrub. But what made it stand out was its whiteness – its cold but startling whiteness almost gleaming in the subdued light

Roger moved a few steps closer to it and then he realized it was a bone.

A white bone lying on top of the primeval mud.

Perhaps some dead animal's carcase had been washed into the space by the flood.

No, he realized with a slow dawning, it wasn't an animal.

The bone was attached to a hand, a human hand now covered lightly with mud, but still obviously the bones of a hand.

The light intensified. The bone – presumably an arm – and the hand now could be seen as part of a complete body – a dirty mound, but unmistakeably in the shape of a human.

Roger didn't know what to do. His first thought was to get away, to get out of the cave, to run.

Running was what he knew about. It was what he had done all his life – every since he had run from that still body floating down the slough just a little upriver from where he was now.

Wait a minute, he thought, could it be Troy? After all these years, poor Troy, unfound, presumed to be floating, floating, floating forever.

But no. The shape of the body – now even clearer with the sun burning away what clouds still drifted by – was too big to be Troy.

The body – or was it a skeleton? - was that of a man, not of a young pre-teen boy. In fact, from what Roger could make out, the shape was tall, taller than he.

Roger knew that if he stayed where he was and somehow these bones would be found he would be implicated. He would be in trouble, so the thing to do was to run. He hardly had any possessions. He could get on his bike and go. Perhaps he could find another place just like this.

But no, he didn't want to go. His whole life so far had been a moving away and then a long, slow, drawn-out return. Somehow he felt that he needed to be here.

But not here – in this dank cave with the remains of some kind of giant man sent up from somewhere by the force of the flood. He would get out, go to the mission, get cleaned up, have some food. Then he would determine what to do.

But as he looked around to see what things he should take with him, he saw – his eyes were drawn repeatedly to the bones – some fragments of clothes lying over the body shape. That would make sense. People die with clothes on. Perhaps if he wiped some of the mud off he could find out something about the body from the clothes. Why he wanted to do this he could not tell. But something compelled him to move to the body, reach down, brush away some now drying mud and grapple with what was underneath.

He felt threads, hardened and woven threads. They had no strength, falling away completely when he reached around the exposed bone. But they were black threads and as he brushed away more of the mud, he realized that they were a part of a jacket or coat. His prying fingers burst through the layer of blackness into some softer fabric. He looked down and saw that it was white, or what had been white before, but now was a yellowing garment of some kind, most probably a shirt.

He probed more. Were there undergarments? No but he hit something hard, something that seemed to be impenetrable. Was it the body's chest? No, it was a strap of some kind, a leather strap. Sure, a belt. A thick, heavy wrap, almost a wide girdle that he could feel encircled the shape of the body.

And as he felt more, he felt what was probably a button, a round, flat, circular object that to Roger's probing fingers had some texture on its flat sides. All at once the button shape came away from the decaying leather.

Roger drew it to his eyes and almost dropped it because of his surprise and – yes – fright.

For the color, now that he could see it, was gold.

It was a golden colored coin.

And as he looked harder, he could see the date – 1886.

And around the edge of the flat face were the words in English – Twenty Dollars

Chapter 24

Along the Slough

In winter from a second floor window in the Consolidated Freight Office, when the scrub trees and bushes have lost their green screen, a section of Sylvan Slough and the Arsenal Island beyond it is visible. But most of the time the view, except of the path, is obscured by the straggling vegetation along the edge.

The Slough is unpretentious – almost a canal running without a twist east and west along the south side of Arsenal Island. It has a barely perceptible current, visible year round, even in winter when the surface doesn't freeze entirely. Occasionally it does freeze in parts, but the moving water underneath makes it difficult to form thick ice, creating treacherous going for all but the smallest creatures.

It is bordered by the path on the land side and undeveloped grounds on the Arsenal side. A 10 – 15 foot slope on both sides leads to a varying, but narrow shore of land which gradually turns to sand and gravel as it meets the water. The slopes and much of the shore area have grown up with a helter-skelter mixture of mostly non-native shrub trees and bushes, with grasses, vines, and other vegetation mixed in.

But on the whole, the Slough is a nice enough channel of flowing water. Take it away from the Mississippi and it would be a respectable river anywhere – even perhaps having a more recognizable name. Sylvan Slough is hardly known – not even to citizens of the Quad Cities. The Green River in western Illinois, a river about the same width as Sylvan Slough, comparatively, is well known to the residents of that area.

And the slough does have fish – and fishermen. Boats are constantly navigating through it, mostly in search of holes or, in many instances, the water at the tip of Sylvan Island where two streams of the slough are joined again. The tip is a gathering place for both fish and those who enjoy gathering them in. Even in the depth of winter a boat or a shoreline fisherman invariably has a line dropped into the river. The fish variety is generally the same as in the main Mississippi – pike, walleye, carp, boomers, with some bass.

Because, perhaps, of its out-of-the way location and its inhospitable shore and sloping sides it is not a real draw for bank fishers. The exception is the expanded swath of water at the tip of Sylvan Island, which at certain times of the year when the word gets out that "they're biting at Sylvan" teems with one fish line after another along the south shore and on the tip of the island. Camaraderie reigns as even path users hear the fisher folk sharing tips with each other. No up-scale fly fishermen ply the area; blue collars and seed caps rule. However when a "world class" bass fishing championship was held in the Quad Cities, much of the fishing was done on Sylvan Slough. Boats worth hundreds of thousand of dollars vied with john boats for choice spots.

In the distance from the second story freight company observation spot the U.S. Arsenal's buildings give definition to the background of the slough. Built of stately cut limestone, for the most part, massive and solid, they form a line of castellated, somber blocks above trees and shrubs. A water tower, prominent displaying "Rock Island Arsenal" punctures the horizon, a silvery flattened globe atop stilted legs.

Within the Armory, massive machines make massive machines, most of them for killing. Historically, artillery has been the Rock Island Armory's forte. In recent years administration and research and development has become more prevalent on the island's many acres. And it still remains one of the entire area's largest employers, with workers – blue collar and white – converging from every community in the Quad Cities, and, obviously, contributing immensely to the area's economy. Congresspeople running for office never ever slight the Arsenal.

But the Sylvan Slough side of the Arsenal Island is a somewhat forgotten part of the place. The massive armament buildings in general are in the middle of the island. The north shoreline with the main Mississippi, historically the first to be placidly settled, has been taken over by prestigious mansions (including Headquarters 1, second only to the White House in Federal residential square footage), and a golf course. But the south shoreline is mostly waste areas of storage and parking, with a few natural acres still remaining. In general, the very edges of this southern section grow without much attention as mixtures of mostly non-native plants.

Winter finds the trees and rough edges occupied by bald eagles in ever increasing numbers, certainly fitting for acreage owned and operated by the United States Government for almost 200 years. The eagles seem to enjoy the relative isolation of the slough area and at times make a winter bike or stroll memorable on the path with as many as 20 to 25 roosting or soaring. Fortunate observers can even hear eagle calls, and observe the swooping and formation flying of pairs in mating patterns.

Right in front of the second story observation window, however, is a more mundane sight – trucks backing into bays, cars pulling up and parking, workers on short jaunts across the pavements. Waste receptacles abound along with the ubiquitous Dempster Dumpsters. It is paved over completely, except for a few tiny areas of scrub grass and weeds.

The view is reminiscent of much historical American industry – factories with their backsides to both rivers and railroads (which quite naturally followed the riverbeds with their flat gradients), built for efficiency not beauty, and using the back areas for either long term or temporary storage of what was eventually either thrown away, recycled, or remains still there.

An artist would tint the area gray.

And the view would be just about the same – even amid the greenery of summer leaves. No one comes here to take in the sights or enjoy it as a part of a vacation.

No one, that is, except for the fortunate few who can celebrate it and glory in its primitive and special beauty – who can bike, walk, run, or skate through its heart and observe the inherent truth of what it represents.

Chapter 25

Bobby - Parents and Past

Bobby Scott, his skateboard under his left shoe, which slowly moved the board back and forth, couldn't get his mind off what he had found out at the library.

His mother had a brother who disappeared. Poof! Just like that – missing and never found. And he, Bobby, hadn't known a thing about it.

Of course, his mother never did speak much about her family. Both of her parents were dead – her dad before Bobby was born, and her mother when Bobby was probably around three. Bobby had to think hard to remember her, and then all that popped up was an arm with a dangling bracelet containing a windmill. The windmill had vanes that moved, spun around. The bracelet was very shiny and made noise when she moved. Bobby remembered standing by her chair and touching the windmill, moving the vanes – fooling with it so much that finally his mother politely pulled him away from the old lady and put him in his room.

When his grandmother didn't visit anymore, Bobby just forgot about her. His mother never spoke about her, and Bobby didn't remember ever going to a funeral. But he guessed that she was either dead or something had happened that mother and daughter never got together again – for what he knew.

He did know that his mother's father was dead. She told him. She said that he died in a barber's chair while getting a shave and a haircut – actually during the shave. The barber almost had a heart attack. At least that's what Bobby's mother told anyone who asked about her father, which admittedly was hardly anyone. His mother never really talked much and had few friends.

But she and his daddy – James Scott – everyone called him Jimmy, although he was really too old to be called that – were pretty cool together, Bobby thought. Oh, they did rag on him every once in awhile – grades, clothes, wasting time on a skateboard, yah, yah, yah. But they never got really hot about it. He did keep his grades up. That is, he wasn't flunking anything even if he did get Cs all the time.

But they didn't rag on each other much either. They were cool – not like parents he heard about from other guys – or from Marie. Her parents, she told him once when the computer teacher was called out of the room and gave them permission to play computer games, had a weird thing going on at meal times. They never spoke to each other. They talked to her, but never back and forth to each other. Not even to say "Pass the butter" or things like that. But they talked to each other at other times – just never at meals. Marie couldn't figure it out.

One time she just blurted out: "What's the matter, why don't you guys talk to each other?" looking back and forth at the two of them.

Her mother said, "We don't? What do you mean? We talk all the time."

Her father said nothing, just looked at his plate.

Marie didn't push it. So they didn't talk at meals. Big deal! They got along pretty well all the rest of the time. So she let it go at that.

Bobby liked that in her. She didn't push things. Maybe Marie's parents were like his mother. They both kept things quiet.

But some of the guys had parents who were really snarfed. So terrible, from the stories he heard, that they shouldn't be allowed to be even close to their kids. And these were good kids, to Bobby's mind. They didn't get good grades, and they didn't take the bull crap that the teachers dished out, but they didn't hurt anyone either. They didn't steal or use girls just for sex, and they had their own code of conduct, to use the words that Mr. Semple used in Government all the time. God, everything to him was "code of conduct." He should be a preacher, not a Government teacher, for Christ's sake.

But because of Mr. Semple, Bobby had found out about his mother's brother – god, he would be his uncle - having disappeared. Everyone had to do a research project about local history in Mr. Semple's class. What a big bore! Go to the library. Find some old books or newspapers. Read this incredibly boring stuff about people long dead. And then just write it down, although you weren't supposed to just copy what you found. Supposedly you got something out of doing it - something of value.

It didn't give Bobby any value. Maybe old people got something out of it because the only people using the local history books and old newspapers in the library were really ancient people – and kids having to do reports.

Bobby at first wanted to do a report on Looney, the gangster who controlled Rock Island way back then. The name got him – this guy was important and he had a name like that? Unbelievable! That's probably what made him get into the gangsters business. Living down – or up to – his last name. But Mr. Semple told the whole class, "No report on Looney. No ifs, ands, or buts – no Looney. He's been done too much. Overkill. Overkill – get it. You have to find something else. Use one of the topics on the list I gave you. They're all OK."

So Bobby started looking for stuff about the Rock Island Armory, which he could relate to since it had been right next to his favorite place on the river – 20th Street. One of the items on the computer search engine said something about a planned renovation to the 1930s building to be made in

1973. It had the Rock Island Argus of May 19, 1973 as the source. So Bobby asked at the desk for that issue, and found out it wasn't that simple. He would have to take a microfilm and put it into a machine in a room off the main room of the library.

The machine at first was fun – you could really make the plastic microfilm reel spin, even if it took awhile to learn how to control it. Eventually he did locate the paper for May 19 and it had a big article about how they were going to start thinking about either spending a lot of money to renovate the old building or tear it down and move the National Guard somewhere else.

The article was continued to page 8, and when Bobby turned to it, he happened to notice a rather small item printed next to the column about the Armory. It told about a Rock Island boy, who went to Lincoln School, being missing. Maybe that's what caught his eye – Bobby had gone to Lincoln.

But the article didn't say much. The boy, Troy Yelkin, hadn't shown up for supper on Friday, May 17, and his parents were concerned. But they thought he might be staying with a friend and they were expecting to be called. But nothing happened, and all day Saturday they became increasingly worried. They contacted the boy's friends, but all they could find out was that Troy was going down to the river to play after school on Friday – something that he did off and on.

But then the article mentioned that the boy had an older sister who was a student at Rock Island High School. Her name was Marcie Yelkin.

The name flew out of the paper into his eyes, his mind, his dim memories. That was his mother! Marcie Yelkin. She didn't use that last name ever. She was Marci Scott. But Bobby vaguely remembered it from occasional talk and from the yellowing copy of her high school yearbook that was in their bookcase. He had paged through it a few times, slightly interested, and remembered being almost astonished at the picture of his mother. She was so young. And her name was not Marcie Scott, but Marcie Yelkin.

And now here was that same name in an article about a missing boy who went to Lincoln and lived in the same neighborhood where Bobby lived.

Bobby made a copy of the article from the microfilm and that evening after supper he asked his mother about it.

"Bobby, it's true. He disappeared. He was never found. They didn't even find a scrap of his clothing."

"Wow! That's something. You mean nobody even saw him after school. Was he a loner?" Woops, did he really mean to ask this? Wasn't he also a loner

His mother replied, "A loner? I don't think so. He had friends, you know. He didn't have any best friend, if that's what you mean. But I was in high school at the time, and I didn't really know too much about what was going on with him."

"He just never showed up again. Whew. That's something. I mean, like, he doesn't come home – any time. Where did he go?"

"I don't even want to think about it, Bobby. It's in the past. And I've spent too much time in my life thinking about it. Especially in high school, it affected me."

"Gosh, I didn't know that."

She hesitated, "Don't tell your father this. I've never told anyone. You're the first. But I lost my concentration. I was a pretty good student in grade school and junior high, but when it happened, at the end of my freshman year, I . . . I just couldn't . . . think about anything else."

Bobby, out of impulse, took his mother's hand, something he never did – at least in the last five years or so, since he wasn't a kid anymore. "I'm sorry."

"I had nightmares. I still do – sometimes. Not often, anymore. But still every once in awhile . . ."

"Nightmares. God. That must be terrible."

Bobby's mother twisted her hand away from him. Without thinking she started rubbing her two palms together, sometimes curling her fingers together into a ball. "It's always down by the river. That's what gets me. The river is always there. Something happened there. I don't know what or how. But it's always the river. I don't like that river, that dark river."

Chapter 26

Jane – Awards Gala

Disheveled tables – crushed napkins slipping over plates, crystal glasses rimmed with traces of lipstick, uneaten potatoes pushed to the side, dregs of wine coating flute bottoms – the "awards gala" was over. And Jane Tressel was still soaring at an exuberant clip.

She was the chairperson of the organizing committee of advertising people who sponsored the event. It was a demanding job, involving long extra hours, unpaid ones, but she still had time to do her almost daily bicycling along the Rock Island riverfront, including the path along Sylvan Slough.

Jane worked at Mechem, Haver, and Beakon – a full service ad agency serving the entire Quad City area, but located in downtown Rock Island. It was generally recognized as the best and most prestigious agency in the five cities. Her title was "executive enhancement representative," but what she really did was act as a middle person between businesses needing advertising and the professional crew of ad producers in-house at her company.

She was very good at her job.

Outgoing but not vivacious – attractive in a somewhat disconcerting way - she nevertheless was a whirlwind of organizational activity when she felt compelled to be. And the event which was now at its end was just one of her compelling bursts. In fact she was the one who started the annual dinner and awards ceremony for excellence in advertising in the Quad City area. She set up the network of likely people and conned them into becoming committee members. She even was the one who named the group: the QC ad-atising. Committee.

And she also named the awards. They were the Quirkys, a subtle dig at the reality that the area consisted of five cities, not the four that the title "Quad Cities" boasted. But the committee applauded the name choice, liking its pixie, off-the-wall reverberation.

Now, when most of the guests either had left or were just about to, she had her first glass of wine of the evening, emptying a half finished bottle of pinot grigio left on the portable bar. The bartender was helping the serving staff clean the tables. While sipping its full bodied goodness – it was a

Rothchild 2008, she chatted with two of her fellow committee members – Rose O'Brien and Keith Mensurth.

Keith was also exuberant. "You did it, Jane. What a great evening. It couldn't have gone better – especially since my agency picked up four of the awards. Oh, we're going to be happy tomorrow. Probably won't get any work done."

Jane replied, "Calm down, Keith, you're always so "up," so vital. And you know what? That makes you fun to be with." She put a hand on his shoulder and gave it a clutch.

He couldn't contain himself. He grabbed her arm and pulled her to him, crushing her in a laughing bear hug. "It was a success. Jane, you really put it together just right. I loved that parody you read in the middle of the animation awards. You're so talented."

Here he pushed her away and almost yelled, "You're so good. You know what? You ought to be in advertising!"

Jane liked Keith very much, but "like" was the proper word. She had no other feelings toward him, just genuine platonic affection. But still he was quite a contrast to her husband, Fred, who compared to the steam ship Keith was dead in the water. He was cool and taciturn, and getting more so almost day by day - sometimes hardly saying a word to her for an entire evening. And lately, he just wasn't around too often in those evenings. Somehow his work – he was a truck parts store manager for a major national company – was taking more and more of his time.

Now all three of them – including the unusually very subdued Rose O'Brien, took a last look around the dinning hall and prepared to leave. Jane caught the eye of the hall's manager and gave an approving nod. The place was in good hands.

The three of them sauntered over to the cloak room. Rose had worn no wrap, but Jane had a light coat hanging on the rack. Keith followed her in, still beaming and gushing about how good the evening had been. He even put his arm around her shoulder and gave her a light kiss on the cheek – really no more that a peck – while saying, "Thank you, Jane. Thank you so much."

It was then that Jane caught just a glimpse of some movement to the rear of the small room, movement behind a curtain that acted as a door to an inner tiny storage room. Her eyes were drawn to the movement and then to a pair of shoes slightly protruding from under the curtain.

They were Moc-a-Step shoes.

Chapter 27

The Armory

A big, arched-roofed structure, the Armory dominated the Rock Island riverfront for years. Nothing else could touch it. Other buildings, mostly manufacturing, didn't come close. Newer building were built, but none had the classic strength and simplicity of the Armory. Some were adjacent to the river, but the Armory was right next to it, almost on it.

If fact, it was almost a part of it. For the Armory's riverside acted as a seawall for the levee. Before the actual levee was built, the Armory loomed along the river, acting as a stabilizer for a key section of riverfront directly north of Rock Island's downtown.

They built it strong in the 1930s. Especially that Armory wall with the river constantly next to it. Oh, they filled in some dirt between the wall and the river, but it was the wall that held back the river when it rose.

They also build it in classic 1930s style: Governmental Art Deco. Its massive front arch, capped by strong bands of layered cement, its platform steps leading to its westward facing entrance. It's huge shape, a monolithic elevation of 40 feet before the arching roof took over, reaching a combined height of 65 feet.

It's not that it was so distinctive – thousands of almost similar armories were build all across the country during the period between the World Wars. Effective make-work at a time of national anxiety, these places were not just about the Great Depression, but also the rising militarism wafting from central Europe. But what made the Rock Island Arsenal distinctive was its location.

At a time when riverfront communities shunned the water's edge, The Arsenal stood proud right on the river, not near it, but on it. It was in command – which was perhaps the image its creators were seeking.

Its simple structure was composed of two main parts, both suitable for military training use, but also compatible for other uses. One part, the dominant one, was a singularly large open space occupying most of the main interior. This was the training floor. A whole regiment of National Guardsmen could be assembled here for both ceremony and work. The space above the floor reached the arched ceiling, making it a compelling open space. The floor, thick concrete, echoed through the years with boots, gun stocks, and small military machines. Here was might and power enough to protect the community, just as the building could protect it from the natural forces of the river.

Below this vast open space, a basement rivaled its upper space for surface. But it did not have the height leading to the roof. This basement space was capped at about 10 feet by the upper floor. It was used, for the most part, for storage space for the vehicles, and other equipment that the Guard used for its training.

But the upper main floor, besides its military use, could also be used for much else. It was an effective indoor arena for expositions, fairs, festivals, and other community functions demanding a large open space. It was the place to go in the winter for an almost weekly series of "Shows:" the Auto Show, the Boat Show, the Dog and Cat Show.

On both sides of the main floor a series of offices, restrooms, and storage rooms edged the open space. These were not high, and they were capped by a common platform that with a railing provided space to look over the main floor. Bleachers could be erected on this platform, at times extending down to the main floor. With the seats in place it could be used for commercial presentations such as ice shows, circuses, even somewhat limited sporting events such as basketball and hockey.

It had a small stage at its east end, and when the floor was filled with folding chairs, it became an effective great hall for political rallies, cultural presentations, musical acts, and theatrical presentations.

In time, however, the Arsenal began falling apart. The National Guard, citing the need for more space, moved to a location far removed from the river – not incidentally building a brand new building for its purpose. This building, however, was hardly as monumental as the old Armory. It was almost indistinguishable from the nondescript commercial buildings bordering on an area outside the contiguous Quad Cities.

The State of Illinois owned the old Armory, but without a dedicated tenant the building fell into fitful use and disrepair. For awhile an amateur soccer team rented it off and on. Sometimes baseball teams practiced there before the snow melted in early spring. But it was allowed to deteriorate. Its roof, in particular, developed leaks and whole sections blew away.

The recreational path was built around it, not traveling along its riverfront narrow walkway where it would be somewhat constricted, and where it would have to deal with a large parking lot and access to a very active riverfront casino.

The city of Rock Island, realizing that the Armory was an important component of its riverfront and in particular its levee system, eventually bought it from the state for a giveaway price. While the city pondered what to do with it, it rented it out to the nearby casino for parking. Where once defenders of their country learned their skills, now gamblers for a few dollars gained inside protection for their cars.

But it didn't last, even though the very solidity of its construction was a daily visual reminder and metaphor for brute strength and power. Not long after the riverboat casino – following the new armory to the outskirts of the community – left the river, the demolition cranes and bulldozers came in. It was hard and difficult work, but the sturdy iconic building succumbed.

An outdoor park and play area took its place. Ironically enough almost all of the functions of the old armory now take place in the space that it occupied – except they are open to the winds, rains, and sun of the outdoors. A key part of the new park is a performance stage with a large viewing area. But no ice shows, circuses, dramas, or the like fit into the new configuration. And absent, of course, is the tread of marching Guardsmen practicing to defend their state and country.

Chapter 28

Bill – meets Jane

His Cannondale road bike cleaned and shined; dressed in his nylon/Lycra moisture-wicking jersey which screamed in red and black the glories of GITAP, a week-long bike ride he did two years before; wearing his 8-panel, black Lycra shorts with coolmax chamois for crotch padding; and his feet encased in Pearl Izui road shoes adjusted for his clipless pedals; Bill was ready.

On this Saturday he was ready to join the bike club for a 60-mile ride up the path and then out into some of the traffic free roads north of the Quad Cities. Bill was a member of the club, The Quad Cities Bicycle Club, but could hardly be called an active member. He paid his dues, read his newsletter, and occasionally joined the club for a weekend ride.

Today's ride was starting at the border of Moline and East Moline, where a large parking lot met the path and made it easy for riders from all over the area to park, get their bikes on the ground, and take off. Not too many biked to the start, but Bill liked to, mainly because he lived fairly close to the path and he liked to think of himself as not dependent on his car.

From his home to downtown Rock Island where he picked up the path, to the stating point was about 7 miles, so Bill knew he had a healthy ride ahead of him – probably in the 75 to 80 mile range. It would be good; he was ready for it.

He had done three rides of about 80 miles this year so far – one longer at the club's annual two-day ride up to Dubuque, Iowa, and back. It was called TOMRV, standing for Tour Of the Mississippi River Valley. The first day of it, a Saturday, was a formidable 107 miles, which included some very healthy hills in Illinois across from Dubuque, Iowa. Now with all his gear and clothing in prime condition, and feeling about the same about himself, he was ready to "put some quality miles on," as one of his early biking buddies always used to say at the start of a ride.

On the straight stretch just east of the downtown path entrance he saw her ahead of him, going east where he was heading. She was wearing her trademark yellow biking jersey. It was her! Bill started feeling edgy. She did that to him.

She was about 500 yards ahead, but she was not going very fast. He started gaining on her, which was surprising since usually she was moving along at a good clip. He kept at his usual pace, wondering slightly if he should modify it so he wouldn't have to pass her. But no, he didn't want to be late to the ride; he couldn't dawdle around too much. And after all, he didn't know the woman; she was just another rider on the path – or was she?

Ahead of him was the entrance to the bike/ped bridge to Davenport, with the pumping station on his right. When Bill was just starting to make the dip to this trail intersections, the woman in yellow had slowed down considerably. In front of the intersection she slowed to a crawl. Bill made a quick decision to stop too, rather than swooping around her. With the slight moisture from the morning dampness, his brakes squealed a bit – and she stopped immediately. Bill almost ran into her.

"Hey" involuntarily popped out of him

"Hey, I'm sick of this. Why are you following me?"

Bill was flabbergasted. Following her, well, yes, he was. But he didn't mean to, or, maybe he did.

"Well, I didn't know which way you were going to go, so I . . I stopped."

"Oh, I don't mean here," she snapped. "That's my fault. I have to make up my mind about going to Davenport or whatever. But you've been following me for days now and I've just about had it. Lay off, will ya?"

Bill looked into her dark brown, almost black, eyes and was taken aback. He didn't know what to say. He literally hadn't seen her in at least a week.

He stared – then the words gushed from him, involuntarily and unpremeditated: "But where have you been? Are you still riding in the morning? I haven't seen you for a week at least. I was getting worried, but then I figured you were probably on vacation, or maybe even got a new job somewhere and moved. Ah . . . I'm sorry, I should shut my big mouth."

"You haven't been stalking me?"

"Stalking? What? Me? I haven't seen you for awhile. Where have you been?"

"What do you mean 'Where have I been?' Who are you and why should you care about where I've been?"

Bill was at a loss. She was right. Why should he care? So he said it: "You're right. Why should I care? No reason. It's just that I've noticed you in the past and . . . haven't noticed you recently. And, damn it, I haven't been stalking . . . or even following or . . . Hey, I haven't even seen you for a week or so."

Just then a couple on a tandem approached from downriver. Bill moved off the path to the concrete around the pumping station. Jane followed him – not far, just far enough to clear the pathway.

With her dark eyes squinted because of the low sun, Jane gazed with curiosity. "You know, you might be right. Maybe you're not the one that I've sensed has been following – or watching, or something like that.

You're . . . too normal. Oh, I'm sorry, nobody wants to be normal. That's the wrong word. It's just that whoever it is isn't normal. Oh, it's very confusing because I really don't know who I'm talking about. I've never seen him close-up."

"Is this guy a threat?"

Close-up to her now, Bill was overwhelmed by her simple beauty. Her jutting nose, flickering eyes, prominent mouth, demure cheekbones, and scattered black hair gave him a sense of the Mediterranean models he had seen in up-scale magazines. Yet she wasn't exactly beautiful. Simple and classic leaped into Bill's mind. Refreshingly uncomplicated and cleansing: real.

She looked down, which emphasized her full black eyebrows and lashes, and almost mumbled: "Listen, I'm sorry. It appears that I mistook you for someone else. Well, I have to go now – to Davenport. I'm sorry about all this. I didn't mean . . ."

"Yeah, I gotta go too. I'm trying to make the club ride – up by the old Case plant. Gotta be there by eight."

"Club ride? Sounds like fun."

"Yeah, they are – sometimes. So . . . ah . . . I'll see you. Oh, hey, I'll keep watch. You know . . . behind you . . . or – I don't know – around you."

Again with downcast eyes – oh so lovely to him, she said, "Yes. Around me. That's better. Around."

Chapter 29

The Flowing River

Flowing. Flowing. Forever flowing.

The River inexorably flowing and changing, constantly moving but forever permanent. Individual molecules of water move from rain or snow to sea water. But the river remains the same.

It ebbs and it floods. Yet it has a usual girth. Eyesight, boating times, bridges: all confirm that regularity. The river is the same – but it's constantly moving and changing.

On the surface, wind whips. Below, current inexorably pushes and pulls. At bottom, silt and mud edge slowly downward, clinging to the bedrock, but not making purchase, not staying.

And it's carrying.

From the little park on 20th Street, within sight of the roiling and smacking of the dam close to the Government Bridge and the ending of Sylvan Slough, it's possible to see many instances of what the water carries. No, not the poisons – the nitrogen, mercury, cadmium, the carbonate compounds, the lead leached from the land, the top soil beaten into minute particles. These are not visible from the tiny resting place. They become one with the molecules of water, assuming its shape and dappled color.

But bigger flotsam and jetsam occasionally dot the surface or just below.

Great fish float by. Some say that the supreme channel catfish, the "King Cat" of the river lives here in the mud close to the river bottom and the great dam, breaking the surface intermittently just to prove it can be done.

Small fish too. Fishermen, sometimes floating beneath the bridges' iron girders, prove that contention.

And ducks and water birds. But all these, although they float, they also return. This is their area, their home, and they have adjusted to the flow. They move against it, just as they allow it to move them – and to bring them life-giving sustenance.

The great inanimate things, however, grind through the convoluted shoots of the dam and compose themselves enough to be visible and placid as they float beneath the meeting of the river and the slough.

Fishing poles. Some with reels attached. Most bamboo, nicked and broken, entwined with line, bobbers streaming behind like dragsters' ballooning brakes.

Scarred branches. Some green with leaves, some completely denuded by the turmoil of the dam and current.

Forlorn fish. Some of them just dead, killed by a stab of a great blue heron, for instance, but not dying until out of reach – after a mad dash of life preservation gone awry.

Waterlogged branches. Some etched with lichens, some complexly debarked and covered with a road map of insect tracks.

Clothes. Some shirts and jeans puffed up with air almost resembling a floating body, some streaming from a snag on a pole or log.

Underclothing. Some stitched with foamy lace in order to bewitch, discarded before a dip or a moonlit flesh slither. Or just dumped along with other worn-out clothes.

Toys. Color-locked plastic beach balls, cheap toy cars broken and twisted, tiny supermarket carts upended, ruined dolls with bleached faces.

Balloons. Some still carrying a bit of air and a string, the river a balloon magnet for miles in each direction.

Milk containers. Some full gallon size, some lowly pints – all heading for the cove of lost milk jugs somewhere beyond the bountiful main.

Cola bottles. Some – most – less than half empty, carrying their cargo of saccharine liquid half submerged like ocean tankers returning from discharging oily cargo.

Packing material. Some – most – of sturdy Styrofoam, irregular angular smooth chunks floating blithely above the current until sun and water slowly disintegrate them.

Alcohol containers. Some encased in Styrofoam. Some lost from clueless cruisers or shoreline strollers, dropping cans and bottles with arrogant nonchalance.

People. Some swimmers. Some floaters. Not many. Most know about the Mississippi's pollution, load of sediment, and unfathomable currents and undertows.

Bodies of people. Some beneath the surface towed along in a surreal dark world of murky substance, some bloated, breaking the surface with a pop, some scouring the bottom weighted down by attachments, some there because of accident, willful suicide, or negligence. But some, because of deliberate and unlikely deadly intent.

And sometimes a blue-gray mist almost effervescent in anxiety, hovering above the surface – just a haze of insubstantial smatterings of possible dark intent.

The River - Flowing. Flowing. Forever flowing.

Chapter 30

Duane – Floating memories

The boy just floated, as peaceful and placid as a drifting fishing bobber. He was belly-down in the water, but his head was turned so Duane Holstrom could see part of it: could see a jagged tear almost to the ear with red fanning out into the slough's water. It kept flowing, kept tinting the water around it, kept leaving a slight trace, a tendril, as it moved down the slough.

The image wouldn't leave him.

And it wouldn't force him to leave. He thought he would. Right after that fatal afternoon in that bright spring he wanted to quit his job at Consolidate Freight, leave the area, and rid himself of his failure to act. His job wasn't going anywhere; he had only a tentative interest in Sally, his occasional dancing partner at the Col Ballroom; and he hadn't taken an apartment – still living with his parents in the home where he grew up.

But he didn't leave; he had that at least. He didn't even search for a new job away from the place that gnawed on him constantly. He stayed and it stayed – forever with him.

He did get married – not to Sally, but to a spry shipping clerk named June who checked his routings in the pick-up room for him. She was a happy girl, gawky and with a head of finely spun hair that even to this day in his memory threw him in a tizzy when it fell upon his chest in bed when she threw her arm around him and nestled close to his collarbone.

And he did move out of his parents' house – but not far away. Before his marriage he bought the Browning's home, about two blocks from his parents, when old Dean and Barb Browning retired to Florida. It was a big house, too big for just him. But he knew that he would be married sometime in the near future – and he was.

But even on his wedding day the floating boy was present. Duane was about to ladle some champagne punch into a glass for his bride, when one of the floating ice cubes, reflecting light from the brightly lit reception hall, became a floating, half-submerged body in his mind. Duane turned away and quietly put the cup down. When he returned to his bride, she whispered, "Weren't you going to get me something to drink?" He didn't know what to reply, but she was pulled away by a noisy aunt from Dubuque and nothing became of it. He assumed someone else got her the drink.

Now almost 30 years after he had seen the boy, he was still in the same job, the same office, the same house – but not with a wife. He and Sally, after a childless marriage and her engaging in a three year affair with a fellow in the office where she was working, had been divorced. She didn't want much, not even the house. In her mind, he just didn't have much focus – much point in doing almost anything. His life had been just like the boy's - adrift slowly with the current, going inexorably nowhere into oblivion.

And to Duane, that was what happened to the floating body – oblivion. It was never found. It could be still in the slough; it could be mired in river mud on a sandbar in Missouri; it could be in the Gulf of Mexico washed by underwater currents and stripped clean by ravaging creatures of the deep.

For Duane it was always the floating boy, but in his conscience and consciousness he knew who the boy was. The day after he had seen the body, the Rock Island Argus reported in a short item that an eleven year old schoolboy named Troy Yelkin had been reported missing by his parents after he hadn't come home the previous night. The next day a front page story related the growing concern about the still missing boy, a student at Rock Island's Lincoln School, and the efforts being taken to find him. His classmates were being interviewed and an attempt was being made to trace his movements on the day he disappeared. One classmate reported that he thought he heard Troy say that he was going down to the river after school, down by the Farmal Plant. No one knew if any other friend was going with him and no one saw him with anyone else. All of his friends could explain where they were on the afternoon in question. Authorities were going to widen their investigation and also conduct a search of the Rock Island riverbank the next day.

No body was ever found. And no investigator ever talked to Duane. If one had, Duane still didn't know what he would have said. "Well, yes, I saw a boy's body floating across from my office window that day and I didn't do anything. I just sat here and . . . well . . . just sat here."

No, Duane couldn't ever admit it, except to himself. He had been cowardly and inept. He knew he should have jumped from his chair, ran to the shore of the slough, yelled at the boy, possibly even jumped into the water to try to save him – to pull his poor, battered head into the safety of the shoreline. And at least he should have phoned the police and also ran up the slough's shore to see if anyone was in the area. But he did nothing. He sat transfixed in his chair and disappeared into a flux of inaction, a web of cloudy lassitude. Later he should have reported what he had seen, even if it was too late to do anything about the bleeding boy. At least the police would have an idea of where the boy was and what had happened to him. But no. Duane just clammed up. Nothing.

Eventually the investigation wound down and the boy's relatives accepted the fact that the boy was missing, presumably dead. But some of them never gave up the hope of finding him alive. The police put it as either a runaway boy or an accidental drowning death. The community through the years forgot about the incident.

But Duane Holstrom never did.

Chapter 31

Bobby and Marie

Bobby Scott liked his computer graphics class at Rock Island High School. It was held in one of the older classrooms on the third floor of the monumental building. Sure, the room was wired for the computers, but not in a perfect grid. The room's arrangement of stations was eclectic – some were against the one wall without windows; some were in a row facing the windows that looked down on nothing but a new brick bridge between two ells which once formed a courtyard space.

Bobby was assigned a station close to the middle of the room by the brisk, pants suited teacher, Miss Bennet. She wore a pants suit every day – different styles, different colors, different fabrics. Jerry O'Brien, unbeknown to her, made up a spread sheet listing all of her different pants suits and kept track of which one she wore ever since the third week of the class. Jerry was an asshole, however, in Bobby's opinion. He never completed any of the requirements of the class, and spent his time fooling around with producing his name and initials in various combinations. And he was a surely fellow, one who never said anything nice, always trying to come off as the above-it-all cynic. It didn't work. The entire class tried to ignore his fulminations.

But Bobby liked the teacher. She had an impossible job of keeping 30 rambunctious kids on task and not destroying the machines in the room. Every so often, after a short lecture or demonstration at the beginning of the class, and as she was walking around the room keeping an eye on the students' progress, she would stop by Bobby's station and take a look at what he was doing.

Usually when he sensed that she was about to stop by him, he made sure he was on task for whatever the lesson was for the day. Most of the time he would not quite finish the required work, saving the ending items for the teacher's possible visit.

His real time was spent with his secret project. Hair. Boys and girls' hair; men and women's, he was obsessed with coming up with all kinds of different hair possibilities.

He would start with a completely hairless three-dimensional drawing of a human head. He found a web site that was focused on artists' anatomy, and had a category of just simply human heads, bald and hairless. The drawing were essentially sexless. It didn't take Bobby long to discover that it was hair that gave sex to a representation of a head – and by extension, to live humans. Makeup played a part, but just a tiny part. A boy became a boy by the way he wore his hair, and a girl's hair turned her into a feminine human being.

Using the standard draw program that was installed into every one of the computers in the class, Bobby would take the plain and neutral head and add hair to it. He was meticulous. Sometimes he brought swaths of digital hair into his drawing from an artists' web site. But most of the time he was the one who drew in the hair, strand by strand, swash by swash.

He became adept at it, almost miraculously so. He could turn a bland drawing of a head into a full-blossomed human presence in one class session, even while doing the classwork that most of his classmates couldn't handle in the allotted time.

But he couldn't hide what he did most of the time in the class from Marie, who sat right behind him and could watch his monitor all the time if she wanted to. She was skinny, had braces, and was a freshman, but Bobby liked her. He didn't think of her romantically, but more as a friend – someone he could chat with occasionally.

"Hi, Marie. What's up?"

"I'm on the website logo design for today. It's pretty cool, don't cha think?"

"Yea, neat. Hey, I know your secret. Bet cha don't know what I know?"

"I bet I do, but it's not my secret. The big secret is all your fooling around with hair on your computer."

"Nah, nah. That's just something I do."

"So what's the big secret then?"

"You're hair's different. That's the secret. What are you doing with it. It's different. You're curling it, aren't you?

"Well, yeah. What's the matter with that. Everybody does it, why can't I?"

"No, no. I like it. You know . . . don't think I'm in-your-face now, but I think it's very attractive. It makes you seem more – more – I don't know, more grown up, more like a sophomore – or even a junior."

"You think so. You really do? I got this box from Walgreens with my baby sitting money and so I tried it. I wasn't sure how it would work out, but – you know – it isn't half bad. In fact I like it."

"You've got nice hair, Marie. It's so dark and smooth. I'm gonna have to draw it sometime. Do you have a picture of yourself – just your head?"

"Hey, silly. Here's my cell. Go ahead take a shot."

Bobby looked around to see where Miss Bennet was before he turned fully around and pushed the button on Marie's cell camera.

To Marie, he said: "Can you sent that to me right here at this computer?"

"I think so. Let me hook this up. Oh, there it is. Not bad, except for the goofy expression on my face."

"Hey, come on. It's not so goofy. You outta see some of the pictures people take of me. My mom shot one once when my mouth was full of chili beans. Yeah, chilli beans. And some of them were falling out of my mouth. That was something."

And something also was what Bobby did with the photo of Marie. In fact he spent a couple of class days on his "Marie Project." That was after he had done the ordinary class work that Miss Bennet set up for them.

When he was finished, he was very proud of what he had produced. A couple of times while he was working on it he half turned around to see if Marie was watching him, but if she was, she was very good at disguising her spying. She was always intent on the classwork assignments – except for the last five minutes or so in the class. Then she relaxed as she saved what she had been doing and gathered her things up for her next class.

"Hey, Marie, wanna see something?"

"Oh, sure. What is it? Another hair picture?"

"You said it. Here, take a look." He scooted away from his monitor, and there it was: Marie transformed into a sleek model – mature, glamorous, and with curlicues of black hair positively shining. It was as if she were in one of the ads in the slick women's magazines, advertising Suave, or Sun Silk, or some other hair product.

Marie almost said, "Who is that?" But then she caught herself and recognized her thin face through the transformation done by Bobby's hair magic. "God, Bobby, you are good. I almost didn't recognize my own self. I look so old, so . . . I don't know . . . so cosmopolitan. It's nice, but it sure isn't me."

"Well, no. It's not you – but it could be."

Just then the bell rang and their conversation ended.

The next day, Bobby downloaded his Marie picture and without the teacher knowing, printed up two black and white copies of it. He gave one to Marie and kept the other for himself, folding it neatly and putting it in the back pocket of his jeans.

Three days later on a day off of school – teachers meetings - as he was lolling around the little park on the river near 20th Street in the morning, he was distracted by a bike stopping and coming in front of him as he sat on the one park bench. The rider looked intently up the path where she had just come, then nodded her head and peered intently across the river towards Davenport. After a few minutes, she took off her helmet and shook her head while running her fingers through her curly black hair.

Bobby was amazed. She was the very image of the picture he had created with Marie as a model.

Bobby took out the printed portrait and was overwhelmed at the similarity of the two – the picture and the bicyclist – the bicyclist who was wearing a plain, but striking, yellow jersey.

Chapter 32

Eagles

An eagle holds sway on the tip. At the very top of a tall cottonwood tree, cleared of leaves in the winter season, the eagle reigns. Nothing escapes its ken.

The eagle is here for one reason: fish

Cold doesn't bother, but ice does. It's impossible to fish through inches of ice, as in the impenetrable woods in the northland, its normal residence, where it builds its great nests, and lays its eggs, and fledges its eaglets

But here, below a dam, where rushing water prevents ice from forming, fishing is possible. And it is easy. For the flurry of water over the dam catches fish unaware, catapults them over the structure, and stuns many of them momentarily. Floating near the surface with consciousness dimmed, they are easy prey.

A swoop from the tree, an eye glint, an instantaneous descent, and the inescapable grasp of talons.

Ironically, these unnatural river dams bring the normally elusive eagles to live for awhile – up to three months - right in the heart of cities.

The tip of Sylvan Island is not the only winter eagle roost in the area. Even more populated with these flying flashes of white and black is the entire shore surrounding the confluence of this slough and the Mississippi itself – right downstream from Lock and Dam #15. Great amounts of water (and fish) flow through and over the dam, resulting in a constant stream of shore birds, gulls, and eagles filling the air as they soar and search before diving for food.

But the tip of Sylvan Island is not just good fishing for eagles. Humans find it attractive too. When the word is out, the boats appear. And shore fishermen along the the slough's edge are no slouch either. At times the tip of this small island just teems with poles and people, all intent on pulling in some excitement, some contentment, some food, some fun.

The place is not easy to find, not convenient to automobiles or boats, and somewhat wild and unkempt in appearance. It's an isolated enclave, a semi-secret refuge for both man and eagle.

Let it be.

Chapter 33

Roger - the Coins

Roger slumped onto the floor of his cave. He ended up sitting in the slowly thickening mud, but he didn't mind. In fact he hardly knew that he was sitting in it or hardly even felt its clammy wetness.

What he did know, in his almost addled way, was that he held a coin in his hand that was different from any coin he had ever owned or felt. This one was bigger, heavier, and golden. And, as he checked it again and again, it was old. More than a hundred years old. What year was the present? Roger hardly remembered. His sense of time had almost disappeared through the years into a limbo of hardly remembered places, seasons, and occasional faces.

Oh, yes. He did remember the cold new year - the last one. It was the beginning of the year 2010. He forced himself to think. This coin he held in his hand, dated 1886, was 124 years old.

My god. It was ancient. It was an antique. And along the bottom edge were the words: "Twenty Dollars."

And it was golden.

What if it were real gold?

Suddenly some semblance of his sense of value came back. He had lost it through the years as he drifted. He worked a half day; they gave him some cash; he spent it. It went – not on booze or drugs or other vices. No, he bought some food, sometimes a place to stay. But mostly it went for time.

Just time. Sitting is a haze, not watching, but appearing to be.

Time was what had value for him. Why? He hardly remembered. It was so long ago. But now time seemed to be getting nearer and it seemed to be getting faster. If he had a clock or even a watch it would be speeding up.

But wonder of wonders. He had an antique gold coin in his hand, and somewhere in the recesses of his past the idea that it had value surfaced, just like the inanimate bones lying in the back of the cave.

Wait a minute. He rose up until he was standing, but still stooping in the low cave. He thrust the coin into the front pocket of his filthy jeans. He went back to the skeleton dressed in broadcloth, leather, and mud.

He searched again for the belt, moving around its circumference until he found a buckle. He drew the buckle's pin through the hole in the leather that was still holding it together. The entire belt came out of the murk like a black flat snake mesmerized by his hand.

He held it in the air and felt its weight. He had never felt such a heavy belt before.

And as he turned it over he knew why.

Concealed between the double thicknesses of the belt were more coins. More gold coins, more twenty dollar gold coins.

He could see them as he pried open the leather sandwich.

He stopped, hardly aware of what he was doing. But somehow he knew that he had to keep on. It was important for him

He would have value. And that value could buy time.

Chapter 34

The Pumping Station

Most people in the Quad Cities have never seen it – the pumping station building on the Mississippi River in Rock Island. They've seen the top floor, but nothing else. Even though it's a relatively pleasant building, somewhat nondescript and ordinary, its location makes it almost invisible. Constructed as it is almost underneath a busy bridge to Arsenal Island that also connects to Davenport, it is lost to motorists' view as they maneuver the bridge's two lanes approaching Rock Island and a traffic light.

Only a relatively few people out of the region's, or even the city's population bike or walk the path which goes right in front of the building. Those that do hardly take the time to stop and really look at it because, again, the path dips here to go under the bridge, and it also is joined by a road providing access to the building. All of this and a railroad crossing close by means path users have many things to be alert to, and that doesn't include noticing the building.

Not that it should be noticed particularly.

It's a nondescript utility building containing pumps used to pull water out of the river for the city's drinking water. It's a station along the way for water use and purification. Much of the building is a large open space with pumps positioned in a sub-basement humming constantly but not loudly.

The building is at the very end of Sylvan Slough but it doesn't take water from it. Instead intake pipes run under the slough, under the tip of Arsenal Island, and end up with an intake port in the pool behind dam #15, right below the Government Bridge. The intake port is deep enough, 34 feet down, to be protected from freezing and not to interfere with river transportation.

Rock Island, like many river cities, but unlike most communities in America which get their drinking water from wells, drinks the Mississippi River water. This water, brown colored and filled with silt, chemicals, and the runoff from millions of acres of farm and a bit of wood land, nevertheless is cleaned and purified competently by the water department – and the water doesn't even taste bad. Some complain at times when the river is in turmoil about strained tastes, and different nuances, but, in general, most that do drink the water do so without complaint.

With more advanced equipment over the years, the building has yielded space, opening itself up to other uses. One recent use is that of an art glass studio. Some of its western spaces have been taken over by a glass blower who produces a wealth of hand-made art pieces. The artist also teachers glass blowing and uses some of the space to display his art to patrons.

But he also is a close viewer of his stretch of the river, following the nuances of the effects of weather and the seasons on both the slough and the tip of Arsenal Island, which lies directly opposite the Station. He and his corps of students have a privileged viewing seat to watch the ecology of the slough.

Other uses for the building's open space have been contemplated – a bike repair/rental station is often mentioned.

Some visionaries have noticed the roof – almost level with the bridge roadway next to it, but also with view lines over the slough to the tip of the Arsenal - as a possible commercial/entertainment site. A summer outdoor restaurant and bar has been mentioned, along with other possibilities that would benefit from a view of the minor slough as it meets the major Mississippi. With the full river not far off in the distance however, nothing has come of these possibilities.

Instead, very likely the building, in its squat, efficient way, will remain quietly humming alongside the path and hardly a blimp on the radar screen of most citizens of the Quad Cities.

Such is the way, perhaps, it should be.

Chapter 35

Roger – Bones and Coins

At the Rock Island Christian Rescue Mission, Roger asked for clothes. He was told that he could make a selection from the storage room filled with discarded paraphernalia, including an accordion, a wire raccoon trap, but mostly clothes. Roger picked a pair of pants, a plaid shirt, a few pairs of underwear and socks – and he found a pair of black leather shoes that fit nicely, if a little bit snugly.

The mission's manager told him with a big grin – he seemed to live constantly with that grin – that he had to take a shower before he could take the clothes.

Roger agreed. And the shower felt good. In fact he felt good all around, better than he had felt in a long time.

Now with his cache of gold coins securely buried where only he knew – not in the cave, but close-by wrapped in a bottom three-inch section of his jeans which he tore off and knotted around the coins. Thirty seven of them to be exact. He had counted them obsessively in the two days since he had found them. Eventually he buried them with care under a craggy bush that split in two as it emerged from the ground. He buried it three feet behind the bush. Only he could find it. In his mind it was safe - unless, of course, another flood rampaged through the slough.

The bones were where he had found them. He finally got up the nerve to look at them closely. With an old muddy rag he slowly wiped away the muck and dirt covering the remains of the body. He found a complete skeleton covered by clothes, masculine clothes. And the clothes were old – especially the waistcoat and vest encasing the body and its inner clothes. The body wore boots and from what Roger could discern some kind of a frilly shirt, almost lacy at the wrists and neck. The pants were dark and heavy, but seemed to be much more baggy compared to modern pants or jeans. He searched the clothes for any possible identification. But nothing was to be found. No wallet, no papers in an inside pocket. One finger had a large – rather gaudy – gem encrusted ring. Roger released it from the finger and examined it closely for initials or any inscription. None. He kept it, however, and buried it with the coins.

Roger made a mental photograph of the clothes before he covered the body with dirt from the entrance to the cave.

He uncovered the head, but not for long. He did not want to look at it in its gleaming white grimace. He covered it with dirt almost immediately.

He filled the space where the body lay with storm debris and tree and bush limbs from around the shoreline.

Now showered, dressed in new – clean – clothing, and with a breakfast of oatmeal and toast in his stomach, he crossed the Government Bridge to Davenport, more specifically the Davenport Library.

It was bigger than the Rock Island one, and with its constant traffic of somewhat scruffy patrons, he wouldn't stand out as much. It was a bright, expansive modern building, unlike the classic Rock Island Library which was almost as old as the gold coins in his cache.

He didn't have a library card – you needed to have local identification to get a card. He had his stolen identification, but that was for poor old Francis Balch of El Camelo, California, and the driver's license and voter's card wouldn't work in the Quad Cities.

But he didn't need a card. He just wanted to go to the reference department and find a book about coin collecting. Roger – no-value-Roger – wanted to find out what his coins were worth.

What he found surprised – indeed, even shocked – him. The 2003 book, Crabtree's Book of Coins, showed an 1886 twenty dollar gold US coin in good condition worth $1,375.

$1,375. He had never had that much money ever in his entire lifetime.

He felt like jumping up and dancing. When was the last time he had felt like that? But he did return the book to the opening in the line of books and with a slight smile on his face started out of the library's airy first floor.

Wait. Two other things. The clothes and how to convert the coin to real money.

For the first, he went to the stacks, which were mostly located in a second story wide balcony around the huge central first floor space. He couldn't find a card catalog, not realizing that none was there, having been replaced by electronic data bases located around the library. Roger noticed them, but didn't think he could use them, not having a library card.

Instead he trolled the stacks looking for fashions or clothes or costumes – anything that would have illustrations of older clothes, men's clothes. Finally he found an illustrated history of clothing through the years. He paged through it, seeking to match his memory of the buried clothes with anything in the pages.

And – presto – there it was: A gentleman from the 1870s, seemingly ready to go out for a night on the town in New York City or Chicago. He was wearing a great waistcoat, loose trousers, vest, and a very ornate white shirt surmounted by a broad black tie. But below the main picture, in an inset, was a small illustration of basically the same clothes but more flamboyant – a string tie, a sturdy pair of boots, and a bewhiskered face with a long, pencil-thin mustache. Below in fine old font was listed: "A typical riverboat gambler of the 1880s."

It fell into place.

Who else would have a need to carry a fortune in gold coins around with him at a perilous time? And didn't it make sense that he could have been a gambler on a riverboat? Was there a riverboat wreck back then somewhere in the Quad City area – or north of it? Or was he waylayed somehow and ended up in the river? Did he just simply have an accident? Possibilities buzzed in Roger's mind. Perhaps he would spend some time in the library trying to track it down. Perhaps a newspaper account could be located. But would a riverboat gambler, if indeed that was what the man was, even be noted or known. Wouldn't the man want to be anonymous? Or piled with aliases?

Roger was at a loss. But, at the same time, he was somewhat relieved. Completely by accident, he had experienced the upheaval of a probable ancient burial. It was most likely a river floating burial with the body somehow captured, mouldered, and buried next to the river through more than a century

And he was recipient of the man's – who Roger started thinking of as simply the gambler – bad luck even though he evidently had considerable riches.

Roger searched the main floor of the library and found a phone book close to the check-out desk. A quick look in the business section under coins gave him three companies in the area that would "buy and sell any coin of any worth," according to one of the companies, Riverview Coin Company.

Roger made up a story as he left the library and started searching for 2nd Avenue and Cody Street in Davenport, where the coin company was located. He was traveling from California (and he had his faked identification to prove it if he had to) to Chicago and he had almost run out of cash – after spending much of the night on the riverboat casino last night.

He had an old gold coin which his California uncle had given him after he had helped the uncle protect his wine grapes during a cold snap three years ago. He didn't want to give up the coin, but, hey, enough time had gone by – and besides he really didn't know the uncle that well so there wasn't much sentimental value.

What could he get for a 1880 twenty dollar gold piece, he asked the demure gray-haired lady who tended the counter at the store?

She looked at his nondescript clothing with a wry glance and grabbed a circular from a drawer. With one eye on him and the other scanning the booklet, she stopped abruptly and intoned: "What condition is it in?"

"Well, it isn't new, but it's not really in bad condition."

"Can I see it?"

"Uh, no. Not right now. I've got it in security back at the hotel . . . in the safe." Roger didn't know where he got these lies, but now that he was out of his years long daze, they seemed to come naturally – and he seemed to know more about many things than he thought possible.

The lady with hardly a second look said: "Can't tell you what it's worth until I see it. But if you come back with it, you be careful. It's valuable."

She looked back down at the circular and repeated, "Yes, indeed. It's valuable."

Later that afternoon after biking back and forth across the Government Bridge and a secret, unobserved visit to his cave - and a little digging into the ground under a shrub in the vicinity – Roger stood outside the coin shop in downtown Davenport with a check for $2,400 hidden in his left front pocket. He also had $200 in cash – ten twenty dollar bills folded and hidden in his right front pocket.

He also had a slight smile on his face.

Chapter 36

Jane and Stalking

It gnawed on her. Something just wasn't right. "Damn," she thought to herself, "I am being followed."

She knew it was true, even if she couldn't prove it. And the guy who she had accused, she was now sure, wasn't the guilty party. She was sure of that. The accusation had leaped out of her involuntarily when he almost ran into her as she slowed at the entrance to the bridge to Davenport.

She hadn't been thinking of him as some kind of a creep when she noticed him behind her on the path. But she had seen him before – a couple of times – one time he even said something to her and she got a good look at him. Not bad: good looking, nice bod, about her age, Cannondale, kind of a high pitched voice, no wedding ring, must live in Rock Island, on the path in the morning, often.

But this guy wasn't stalking her. He just sounded too honest for that, and besides she could sense a kind of integrity coming from him. Perhaps his somewhat strained voice; could be the way he had to search for answers when she accused him; maybe even the flex of his slim arms – whatever, this man wasn't lying. She was sure of that.

Where did he say he was going? Some club ride. Must be the bike club. She had heard they had rides all the time, all year round. It might be fun to do one of them sometime, but she didn't know any fellow riders who went on them, so she didn't feel right in just showing up. She didn't know the protocol. One of these days she would have to find out more about the club and the rides – maybe ask the personable owner of "Bike One" who took care of her bike.

It was funny but she wasn't embarrassed about accusing the man of following her. After all, technically he was behind her. And maybe she did stop deliberately just to see what he would do. A stalker probably would have gone around, not wanting to be noticed. This guy was just the opposite. He seemed to want to talk to her, to banter back and forth, perhaps even to miss the start of the ride he was heading for. That didn't seem like the actions of a stalker.

Oh, well, he was gone and she was back from Davenport. She had no particular reason for going over there, except to use its riverside path. She did this occasionally, but she didn't like it as much as the one on the Illinois side. Some parts of Davenport's were really little used roadway, not paths - much of it being paved many years before the idea of a recreational path close to the river became current. The service roads for riverfront entities simply had been incorporated into the path concept. Neat and cheap, but not as easy to use as a path that was closed to motorized traffic. Although, to be sure, some recently constructed segments were pretty nice – close to the river, some natural elements, and no vehicles.

The old business downtown of Davenport was away from the riverfront, separated by a railroad and a very busy highway. Despite the building of a very expensive pedestrian bridge across these two arteries, still not much interaction between the two locations took place. Actually, the walking bridge, which cost multi-million dollars, herded people in a beeline between a hotel with its parking lot and Davenport's floating riverfront casino

They built this bridge without bicycle access, and the decidedly unfriendly streets in the old downtown insured almost no bicycle interaction between the downtown and the path. What bikes used the path usually entered the system at other places.

Jane rode south past the baseball stadium and then through a cleared area, called a park, but hardly so – except right along the river where it was nicely groomed. The rest of the space was either parking lots, a kids' play area, or extensive tracks of empty space. In winter snow crews dumped loads of snow here, giving some visual variety to the wasteland before it turned to grimy melting slush. Davenport paid for extensive and expensive plans for the area, but somehow never did anything much with them, except assign them shelf space in the city planner's office.

She turned around after looking at her watch and estimating how much more time she wanted to spend on her bike this morning, which was becoming very sunny and pleasant. However she had other overriding concerns and some errands to do, and she did plan to attend a charity talent show in the afternoon. A girl in her office was going to sing and dance and she had helped her add some more interesting moves to her performance during lunchtime all week. Gladys really hadn't much talent, but she was game enough and a funny fellow worker.

When coming across the Government Bridge she again thought of the guy who took her impromptu accusation earlier. Now she was a little ashamed. God, she shouldn't have been so abrupt, but it just blurted out of her mouth without her thinking. Or maybe she was thinking, because she knew at gut-level that someone was watching her. She wasn't sure if there was danger to it or not, but it was not pleasant – and she didn't like it. If she continued to feel it, or if she saw some concrete evidence, it would make her change her daily routines and she didn't want to do that. She wanted things to continue the same.

Carefree and unconcerned.

She wanted to be not thinking that she had to look constantly in her mirror, not being semi aware of eyes following her, not feeling the compulsion to having to suddenly stop and abruptly look around.

She had no real obvious reasons for her anxiety. Nothing except quick, evasive movements in the periphery of her vision. Nothing except flashes of reflected light on sunny days. Nothing except being concerned about her clothing not being provocative.

Oh, she knew she was relatively attractive. That was something she lived with all her life. And she knew how to deal with it in almost every situation. But this was different. This was at-the-edge, but not quite so. It was a second skin that she wanted to zip out of, like taking off a Lycra jersey. This was something that magnified her beauty making it loom larger than it really was.

As she flew across the Sylvan Slough Bridge, that last feeling – of her beauty enlarged – suddenly merged into a memory of the man who stopped behind her at the start of her ride. Could he really be her stalker?

She turned the 90-degree corner and took the ramp from the bridge down to the path, rolling smoothly into the riverfront area near Rock Island's downtown. But a glance into her handlebar mirror distracted her. Something was back there, way behind her but close to the ramp she had just used. Was it someone on a bike or someone walking. She couldn't be sure.

She could stop right there, but to her right was a small park, more just a resting place than a park. With a quick decision, she turned into it and stopped, turning around to study where she had been.

Nothing.

She could see no movement, no person, no animal. Nothing.

She looked over the river to Davenport, but as she was turning back to look behind her again, she saw some movement on the bike/pedestrian bridge over the slough. A person in a dark outfit was biking across it, away from Rock Island to the path across the Arsenal.

Was this who she had noticed? Just an ordinary person going from one city to another. He or she could have got on the bridge from a street leading from Rock Island. He or she had to use the path for a short distance before making a 300-degree turn around to go up the ramp and use the bike/ped bridge.

Was she paranoid? Was she seeing every person on the path as a threat to her? This was ridiculous. She was too in-control and mature for this, for acting like a sophomore in high school.

She dismissed the whole subject as she looked around to see if anything was in front of her or on the narrow path leading from the park to the main trail.

It was then she noticed the young boy who was sitting on the bench. Why hadn't she noticed him before? He didn't make a sound, but that was not unusual. Why should he? He was just a kid with a skateboard taking a break and watching the river.

He had something in his hand – a piece of paper. She couldn't tell what it was, except that it had deep folds and was clear of any writing.

On a whim, she said hello to the kid. He looked up from the paper and smiled. He was about to say something, when the paper he was holding slipped out of his hand. It fluttered to the pavement before he could retrieve it.

But it gave her a chance to see what was on it.

It was a picture of her. A glamorous picture of her.

She lost a bit of control, and without thinking, took off, away from the boy, but now even more troubled in her mind.

Just what the hell was going on here?

Chapter 37

Sylvan Island

So what do you do with a man-made island that exists because waterpower was an easy and inexpensive way to generate electricity at a time when power demands were just beginning to increase? The water around Sylvan Island was dammed to provide power for the myriad activities at Arsenal Island – and also – to some worrywarts - to keep the Mississippi from changing its channel when the big Lock and Dam was constructed. That dam created a pool of water, which if it hadn't been contained with the smaller power dam on Sylvan Slough, could have worn its way to a new channel. Gravity will out. Water, held back, will find a weakness and pour forth with a vengeance.

So the smaller dam was a two-way benefit: both power and pool protection. And both of these were important enough, and economically justified at the time, for another power dam to be built in the same area. This dam, along with its channel, created Sylvan Island.

So what do you do with this piece of piece of flood plain now cut off by an outlet channel of water?

One use was to mine gravel from the rich bed of limestone just under the surface of the island. The mining created a quarry, still in existence, although partially filled through the years. The gravel was floated away on small barges on the slough, but workers needed access to the island, and of course heavy equipment occasionally was needed – hence a one lane bridge across the lower slough was constructed. It is still there, blocked off to vehicular use, but open, until structural damage caused by no maintenance shut it down, to fishermen, pedestrians, nature lovers, and bikes, especially mountain bikes.

Another Sylvan Island use was for ice – also important at the beginning of the industrial age before cooling and freezing equipment was available. The mined quarry had no outlets, having to be constantly pumped to eliminate rain and snow melt. The water captured by the slowly expanding excavation was relatively clean, however. When the mining ceased, so did the pumping. It didn't take long for a pond to form, water untainted by the waters of the river, encapsulated in still intact impervious limestone. It was just the place for mining ice – no currents and fresh, good water. Thus was established the Sylvan Slough Ice Company, with two buildings, now gone, and a fleet of delivery vans located off the island.

But the major use for the island was for steel shaping and manufacturing. Republic Steel, in the late 1930s, realized that the Quad City area had an abundance of heavy industry that depended on major metal fabrication and materials – and that produced much metal waste. The company set out to capitalize on those two facts, and they came up with what was basically a melting operation using scrap iron and steel. The location: Sylvan Island.

Of course with metal of that weight and of the volume they had in mind, more than a one lane bridge was needed to transport the raw material and the finished products – along with coal to stoke the metal melting cauldrons. Consequently they signed contracts with the Rock Island Lines for a railroad spur on a bridge into the island close to the lower power dam.

Quickly the island became fully accessible and the steel plant up and running. It was quite an operation, involving about 5 acres of land, and numerous buildings, loading docks, and stock containment areas. For about 20 years It operated with good, if not great, success. It employed around 50 men and a few women, and was an early example of recycling. But, like many aspects of industry in the Quad Cities, indeed in the whole country, the era of large-scale metal production and formation came to a head and foreign production nipped it off.

The plant fell into less and less production, finally giving up its ghost in the early 1950s. Most of the machinery was removed, along with anything else serviceable, but the buildings and the infrastructure of the plant remained. Eventually even the railroad spur was removed, but the railroad bridge still remains, coming to an abrupt halt just over the rushing waters of the slough's dam.

The land, deemed worthless, was just left. It became deserted, hardly protected, not even by fences – so few people wandered into the island. Fishermen used the outer edges, but the interior quickly was taken over by the forces of Mother Nature. The island became an urban jungle, an almost impenetrable thicket of weeds, vines, brush, and unwieldy trees. The buildings fell apart, their stone and concrete foundations still in place, but also eroding away. Wildlife found it and prospered. Groundhogs, possums, raccoons, some deer, and even fox, shared the island with a bewildering variety of birds – many resting there in their migrations up and down the Mississippi Flyway – but many taking residence in its flood plain fauna.

The island lived up to its name – Sylvan – to a certain degree. It wasn't a Grecian expanse of woodland tranquility, clean, neat, and populated by all manner of imaginative deities. But it was wooded and wild, a rough variety of woodland, unique because of its location amidst a heavily populated area.

Its glory was that it was forgotten. No one took possession of it, used it, or cared about it. It was allowed to go its own way with no assistance from man, except for an occasional inspection of the levee along the north side of the island, and the occasional Arsenal official checking out the island side of its power plant.

Sylvan Island – a forgotten remnant of a primitive and more innocent past – had no identity, no community consciousness, and no future.

No future – except for kids. And they loved it.

Chapter 38

Roger finds a Room

Roger went looking for a place to stay. He had cash in one pocket, a big check in the other, and 36 more gold coins safely hidden away.

But, now that he had a taste of money – of value – he grew possessive. It was as if a film escaped from his eyes and mind. Before he just accepted what money he acquired with flitting respect. He needed almost nothing and somewhere, somehow, he would survive. It had always worked out that way. He wasn't comfortable, by any means, but what was comfort? He didn't really have a concept of it – at least for the last recent years.

Somehow he realized that he needed to better protect his golden treasure. A bank would be the perfect place. Out of the blue came the knowledge – learned somewhere - that people could rent boxes in a bank's vault, boxes specifically designed for keeping valuables safe.

But he with no resident, no home, no address – how could he get one of these boxes?

He had an identity, the California certificates and papers stolen from a destitute and now dead inmate, Francis Balch, at Acorn Institute, a rehab center, where Roger shuffled through the office as a part time helper in the distant past.   But he doubted that would be enough.

He needed a place to live. He mounted his bicycle and went back across the river to Rock Island. He knew that he had to live in Rock Island. Something drew him to it.

He walked into the old fashioned Rock Island library, searching for a newspaper. Close to a series of long, wide tables he found a kiosk filled with newspapers, one of them just what he wanted: The Rock Island Argus.

Searching through want ads, he soon found the "Sleeping Room for Rent" column. He really didn't want a complete apartment; all he needed was a furnished room – and he found a list of them. One, on 21st Street and 7th Avenue, caught his eyes with the phrase, "inexpensive and close to downtown, small kitchenette."

With nothing to lose, he biked to the imposing old house located across a busy street from the playing field of a meandering school a block away.

The man in charge, who came after he had to repeatedly knock on the door, was brusk but eager to rent him a room. He could have a room on the second floor for $50 a week. He would have to share a toilet and bath. And, after the landlord saw the bicycle parked next to the house, he could use a bike parking space in a locked back room in the basement.

Roger was interested. They went up the dusty back stairs to a long hall of closed doors. The landlord unlocked one and ushered Roger in. Just a bleak room with a bed and mattress covered now by a decidedly gray sheet; a crumbling sofa, stained with various markings; a wooden chair next to a metal table with a slightly rusty top surface; and a rudimentary kitchen in a corner – a sink, a tiny refrigerator. and a small gas stove. A counter above it held an jumble of dishes, pots, and one frying pan.

In contrast to the seedy look of the room was an authentic, but closed off, fireplace complete with a dark wood mantel. Above the mantel was the only window for the room – with a square glass pane surrounded on all four sides by a framework made of bits of colored and leaded glass

But on the whole, the room was just about as basic as to be had. To Roger, however, it was something out of dream – or a dim memory.

He jumped at the chance to rent it.

The man led him down to a big kitchen on the first floor, where he had Roger sign a rudimentary form of lease for $50 a week, one week at a time. He also asked for a $50 deposit for any damage that might occur.

Roger pulled out five of his twenties and signed the papers.

He now had a residence.

And that meant that he could now rent a box in the big vault of a bank.

Chapter 39

Crossing the River

Crossing over the Mississippi River from Rock Island to Davenport through the U.S. Arsenal is daunting – whether by train, car, bicycle, or even foot.

Part of the trouble is that the crossing is old, and was built for a much more sedate time. The actual bridge itself is over a hundred years old, which gives it a classic image, even if it is by no means beautiful. That could be qualified. An engineer studying the intricate network of interlaced struts, rods, and plates might marvel at the economy of the design. But when we're used to soaring, gently curving structures built more recently, this bridge gets credit for simple utility rather than beauty. It doesn't soar – in fact, it's flat, almost parallel to the river and not much higher than the highest flood stage of the water at this point.

It can be so low to the water and still handle both hulking barges and many tiered riverboats because part of it is a swing bridge. Pivoted in the middle, it can make a complete 360% turn-around, in the process letting the tows push their barges through the opening when the bridge is parallel with the current. Of course this means that cross traffic is brought to a standstill. Barges, by long-standing custom and law, take precedence. No one questions this anymore, even in this era of declining barge traffic and mounting car traffic

The passage between the two cities is further complicated by the fact that it involves not just the swing bridge, but also two other segments. One is about a half mile of roadway on the Arsenal Island itself, complicated by two entrances to the federally protected and security conscious island. Generally the road moves vehicles easily, except when heavy Arsenal traffic backs up.

The other segment is another bridge, this one over Sylvan Slough. Because only small boats can use the slough, it also doesn't rise much over the level of the water. The bridge's two lanes, one in each direction, make for slow and compounded traffic at times.

Essentially the whole bridge system here was built for workers on Arsenal Island. Separate entrances close to the ends of the bridges allow passage to the main island. No reason, except simple efficiency and history, caused the roadway between the bridges to be built – making this somewhat complicated passage a way to move between the two cities, Rock Island and Davenport. Although the U. S. government owns the bridges and the land between them, people use them freely almost as a right conferred upon them by long usage and the passage of time.

Most don't even mind the delays caused by towboats and Arsenal workers going or coming from work.

Both bridge entrances on either side act as true tests of Quad City living. The directions and signage – decidedly difficult to understand and use - are ignored by everyone except visitors or tourists, who usually figure out where to go only after a number of tries.

Recently a bike-pedestrian passage has been added to the slough bridge and with the widening of the former sidewalk between the Arsenal's two bridges, bicycles and pedestrians now have a traffic-free means to transit the river. And the transit connects with paths along the river on both sides.

Now bikers and walkers are on an equal level with vehicles in navigating this difficult crossing. Actually, they have it even easier – since the entrances are directly connected to the paths on both sides, unmarred by confusing signs and directions.

Who would think that bicyclists would be able to cross the Mississippi River easier than motorists?

Chapter 40

Duane – Path Watching

Eagle eyed Duane Holstrom loved the last two hours of his shift. The usual in and out truck traffic slowed down, sometimes to almost nothing as the drivers took pains to get their deliveries done before night. Many of the local ones made predominately daily trips to locations in the Quad City area.

But even if traffic continued at a daytime pace, Duane still had time and opportunity to do what he really liked to do: watch Sylvan Slough and its path. Over the years, and with the sometime help of his binoculars, he had learned the nuances of the path's evening use. And he even made up imaginary names or nicknames for the users.

He knew that a racing team of three blue-jerseyed riders would come speeding up the path, almost precisely at 6:15 every evening. The blue Tribe

He knew that his two favorite walkers, a black man and a white man, both elderly, would command the bench overlooking the merging waters soon after 6:00 o'clock almost every evening. The black man had recently taken to using a cane, but it didn't seem to stop his almost daily walks to the bench. They would stay for about 15 minutes before moving to the path entrance near the Sylvan Island foot bridge. Ebony and Ivory

He knew that a police car would pull up between 6 and 6:30 in the lot adjacent to his company's space and that the cop would sit there for at least 15 minutes, busily pursuing either a newspaper or a magazine and usually munching on something – usually an apple, but sometimes a sandwich in a paper bag. Lazy Copper

He knew that a group of teen-aged boys on skateboards usually would take over the small park bench as soon as the old men left their place. They seemed to be merciless and deliberate in trashing the bench – but it held up under the strain. The Mashin' Bashin' kids

He knew that at 7:00 a man on a black bike would stop at the small park next to his building, walk into it, and take a piss. Urnation T. Clonghorn.

He knew that three times a week, two middle-aged ladies would emerge from the Moline entrance of the path. They would be carrying binoculars around their necks and have books and notepads in hand. Birdwatchers. The Titmice

He knew that at different times three couples, invariably walking hand in hand, would pass his bridge – back and forth – during the course of the evening hours. One couple in their 20s, another probably in their 30s, and the other at least 70 years old. I Wannas, as in "I wanna hold your hand."

He knew that one man in a motorized wheelchair would zip along the path and pause for a breath near the park bench about 6:30. The pause also included a swig of something in a bottle wrapped in a paper bag. Bottle Power

He knew that another man, walking as forthright as a stalker, also carried a wrapped bottle and took great gulps from it even as he strode. Swigin' Power

He knew that an obviously homeless man called the area his home. Usually he could be seen sitting close to the water on a beached log, pack next to him, staring out at the river. The Sad Sack

He knew that on every Tuesday and Thursday at about 7:00 a large number – sometimes as many as 40 – of bicyclists would be riding together, their jerseys a kaleidoscope of color and movement. The Rainbow Fleet

He knew that if he didn't get a good look at someone going by, all he had to do was wait because almost everyone went back and forth on the path.

He knew individual cyclists and runners, the most numerous users of the path, if they exercised with any degree of regularity. Their bicycles, their clothing, their gaits, their speeds, the places they stopped, even their hair styles gave them identity to Duane.

But the one he knew the best was the one who often wore the plain yellow jersey. He called her very simply, "Yellow Bird," and he was in love with her - so much in love, he was beyond infatuation into almost compulsive obsession. He knew he would never do anything about it. In her long distance dignity, her grace, her clean beauty, she was an icon of delight to him.

He knew she was unapproachable to him. That really didn't matter. He was used to a life without love, without even companionship. He, a 57-year-old man who did nothing with his life but roam between his obscure and isolated job and his dingy three room apartment down a gray and crestfallen Rock Island street in the old section below the bluff of the river, knew he had no chance of affinity to the dark haired beauty whom he saw many evenings.

And those evenings when she bicycled by – especially when she was alone, which was most of the time – became the high point of Duane Holstrom's life. He grew to the point where he could almost sense when she would appear, riding always up river and always on her light yellow Trek road bike. He knew the bike, not from its name printed on the bike's down tube, his binoculars were not good enough for him to make it out.

No, he had gone to the biggest bike dealer in town, Jerry and Sparky's over in Davenport, and almost immediately had identified one sitting on the sales floor just like the one she rode. Just like that, it became the best bike in the entire world to him. When the salesman approached him, he asked – almost demanded – its particulars and price. He left with a brochure, which featured the bike along with others of the same type.

She didn't even have to wear her trademark yellow jersey. Duane came to know her figure and her image, without the need for superficial artifacts such as bike, helmet, or even her closet of yellow clothes. She was imprinted on his memory, his consciousness, the very heart of his life.

He made sure he never missed her.

Chapter 41

Roger – his food, his Memories

Roger had just done something that he hardly knew he could do. He had cooked himself a meal. In biking around the neighborhood of his rented room, he had found a grocery store, Save-a-Bunch. It was bright and clean and with an attractive array of products, most unknown to him.

But he did notice a package of spaghetti dinner. Called Best-A-Roni, it had "everything you need for a tasty Italian spaghetti dinner." He looked carefully and saw that you did have to add a can of concentrated tomato paste. But the package looked good. He bought it and the paste – and on the way out noticed a loaf of Italian style, hard crusted bread.- so he added that to his purchases.

He did have one problem. How could he carry the food on his bicycle? He had no bike basket or panniers, and no backpack. The store, a franchise of a minimally priced chain, did not give out throw-away plastic grocery bags. They did sell more substantial ones for ten cents.

After trying to figure out how to bike while carrying the purchases, he took the advice of an old man leaving the store, and went back in and bought one of the bags. It became his constant shopping companion.

Back home, he opened the box and found it consisted mostly of hard strands of dried spaghetti. But also inclosed was a packet of spices and another packet of Parmesan cheese. Roger read the directions on the back of the package closely. He would need two pots, one for the spaghetti water and one for the sauce. But the room's kitchen had only one pot, a fairly big one, big enough for the spaghetti and its water.

The kitchen did have a frying pan, and Roger figured it would do to heat the sauce. But another problem loomed. How did he open the can of tomato paste? He searched the drawer in the counter where the utensils were and amid the various battered piece of silverware found a can opener. It was one meant for opening soda or beer cans, but eventually with many stabs and piercings of the can, he managed to fold back the lid and get at the pungent paste inside.

The sauce was a snap to prepare – and it was pretty tasty, as Roger knew by tasting it as it cooked on the one burner of the stove. When it was hot, he replaced it with the pot filled almost to the top with water.

While waiting for the water to boil, Roger indulged – besides, he was hungry – in hunks of the crusty bread. He ripped open the cheese package and sprinkled a little on the bread. Ah, delicious!

Soon he was enjoying the first home made meal that he had ever cooked – as least in any memory that he was able to bring back. The spaghetti was good, if a bit soggy, but the sauce and the bread added enough spice and texture to revive a memory of food almost forgotten during his years in a daze.

Now he sat back on the sofa, feeling good even with its spring coils moving beneath him. With the spaghetti sauce flavors filling the room, Roger, almost uncontrollably, started remembering things from his past.

A gym class at Rock Island High School. Six weeks of swimming. Dog paddling down a lane between plastic ropes held up by small buoys. Looking over, not one, two, but three lanes over – a body. Not moving. Just hovering. On its front with head turned. Its face staring right at him. Its face, surrounded by wisps of weak red tendrils, ghastly white and puffed. And to Roger, unmistakeably so.

Jane, his sister. On stage in the big auditorium. Emily in "Our Town." She, sitting in a straight-backed chair, looking straight ahead. George, played by Ben Harper, a smart-Alec from his Geometry class, falling down in front of her. She, not moving, just staring ahead with a slightly puffy expression on her face.

Walking to class at the University of Illinois in Champaign. Hardly noticing the stream of hurrying students going in the other direction. A flash of white. One approaches. A face of white. Pudgy cheeks. Mouth slightly open. Eyes blank and filmed over.

A dorm room at the U of I. No one else in the building. Class time on a Wednesday morning. Staring at the wall. A poster of a basketball player gliding effortlessly through the air, large leather ball hovering just above his upraised hand. The ball player floating, floating, never stopping, never coming to rest.

Acorn Institute. A circle of people of varied age and sex. A girl his age seated next to him. Her wrist on the arm away from him scarred. She picks at it with her other hand. Droning voices. No meaning. Just a buzz. He not speaking. A buzz.

His room at the institute. Sitting on his bed. Just sitting. Hardly moving. Staring at the window, covered with a filmy curtain that blows in the soft California breeze.

Dr. Curran. Holding up a paper from a test. Many checks, but no red. The doctor nodding and smiling. "How'd you like to help us out here?"

The institute's office. Taking inventory. Papers all over the desk. Computer and keyboard; his fingers floating over the machines. Many check marks; no red.

Mrs Sourcer. "Here, Roger, please put these in order. They have to be done today, and I just don't have the time. You can do it easily; you're good at it. You're a good bookkeeper." Personnel files. Everybody there. He's there – Roger Pice. His whole record.

Mrs Sourcer: "Roger did you hear about this morning. Fran died. Yep! Just like that. He never woke up. I don't think he had any relatives, but you check on it. Will you? I've got to go to the luncheon over at the Highway House. They're having a speaker from the state medical department. I've got to be there. So you take care of it, will you, please?"

Francis Balch No surviving relatives. No funeral funds. Send death report to: California State Information, Central Records. All information must be kept on file in permanent records.

Francis Balch . . . Roger Pice . . . Francis Balch . . . Roger . . . Francis . .
.

Mrs Sourcer: "Roger, look at me. Put that ledger aside and look at me. I have something important to tell you. Roger, I just got a letter from Rock Island, Illinois. It's from a bank there, the bank that has been sending money to keep you here at the institute. Roger, they can't send any more money, well, because . . . because – well, your father died. He's dead, Roger. He was in a car accident. Roger, I'm so sorry, real sorry You are a good worker and I'd like you to continue working in this office, but – well – that bank in Rock Island had to stop sending in checks for your upkeep here. Your father's estate is in probate and their hands are tied. I don't know what to tell you. But you're going to have to leave. I don't know, maybe you can go back to Rock island. Do you have any relatives there? How about your mother? It says you have a sister . . . named Jane? Have you kept in contact with her? You've never mentioned her. Just your father – through the bank in Rock Island, the First Security Bank. You should go back, Roger. If you can't make the funeral,you need to be back for the estate – if there is any."

Fredericksburg, Texas: "Hey, you, buddy, ah, Roger. Quit staring off into space and bring up another pack of those green shingles. Come on, get moving. Hey, wait a minute. Where you going. Hey, you can't just off and leave. We're in the middle of a job here. I gotta have some shingles up here . . . "

Corpus Christy, Texas: "Yeah, but if you want to stay here overnight, ya gotta do three things: Number one, ya gotta go to the prayer service- it begins at 5:30 sharp. Number two, ya gotta take a shower before you can even touch a bed. Make sure you get a confirmation slip after you shower so you can show the dorm man. You don't have one; you don't sleep here. And three, No drugs and alcohol. Don't let me catch you with any of those, or you'll be gone as fast as a quarter in a slot machine."

Butte, Montana: "Hey, guy. Don't you see that cart out there? You can't leave a cart all by itself out on the lot. Mr. Sam, he wants a clean parking lot. No, no, no. Sam Walton, he's dead, but we like to joke around and say that he's the boss around here. He's the one who started this big deal, this big store. And he demanded a clean parking lot. Got that? So go out there and round up every one of those carts. And check the cart stations too. If they're about three quarters full – or say a few more or less than that – then you gotta bring 'em in to the cart room. Got that? Round 'em up and bring 'em in. Just like the old West, right?"

Mosine, Alabama: "You got anything in that bag there, Man? Come on, open it up. If you're gonna be one of the bridge guys, you can't keep no secrets. Least ways food and money, that is. You got secrets of the heart, that's OK. And the Law. Better fess up. If the bulls are after you, we don't want no part of it – or you. You can sleep here, but you gotta open up, you hear. You gotta open the bag."

Crested Horn, South Dakota: "Hey I give you a ten so you better give me some change. It's right there. See it. That ten right there. I give it to you for this here can of Pepsi and I want my change. That's what I came in here for – to get some change. So gimme it."

Chester, Illinois: "Excuse me, but is anyone sitting here? Is it all right if I sit here? None of the other benches are open. And I like to sit here in this park and just enjoy the afternoon. You know, just sit and watch the Mississippi. It's so pretty from up here. Much prettier than down there close to it. It smells once you get close to it. And there's some awful nasty things a-floating around in it. What do you think? You spend any time down there close to the water? Say, you from around here? I don't believe I've seen you around here before. You just visiting or what?"

Memories float, shimmering away, convoluted and elliptical. Roger opened his eyes wide. He hadn't been sleeping, but he wasn't really awake either. But he was in the dark – his tiny room a black cave – yes a cave, but not moist and unruly. The room was neat, he could tell through the deadly dark.

He was content.

He surprised himself by being content.

Chapter 42

Schwiebert Park

Rock Island, through adroit political maneuvering during the times of its economic downturn – it lost big factories – International Harvester, Case IH and even lower production on the Rock Island Arsenal – acquired one of the ten gambling franchises allowed in the state of Illinois.

At the time, in order to sell this "sinful" activity, gambling was only allowed to take place on riverboats. So Casino Rock Island, a riverboat with some supporting vessels, appeared on the riverfront, just north of Rock Island's downtown.

The Armory building, in bad repair, did have a parking lot to its west, and that became the entrance to the boat, which could be permanently docked to the flood protection levee at this point. In fact the Armory's river-facing foundation formed part of the levee.

As the years passed, Jummers, the company that owned the casino boat, realized that because of its location it was "missing the boat." Two other riverboat casinos also operated in the area, within three miles of each other. The most productive in terms of earning was one just a few blocks from an exit on an interstate highway.

The management of Jummers, with not much of a gamble, got permission to move the casino license and build another casino in Rock Island, but at its extreme southern edge and hardly close to the Mississippi. It got permission to not be a boat, just a glitzy, pseudo Las Vegas expansive building, filled, for the most part, with slot machines.

That left an empty space along the river in downtown Rock Island. When permission was finally granted to demolish the deteriorated Armory, more space opened up.

Just the place for a new riverfront park.

The wheels started turning and – presto – Rock Island in the summer of 2010 had a finely crafted park, certainly not as large as the one across the river in Davenport, but one of human scale and also filled with various options.

Kids had a wet-blast playing at a imaginative water park and playground.

Small performance groups tooted and emoted on a stage before a grassy audience area.

Seat level boulders allowed strollers along a walkway next to the river to take a rest and in winter to view the eagles flying around the tip of Arsenal Island.

Some public art settled into appropriate places.

The established bike path didn't go through the park, but bicyclists could detour from the path for a pleasant, and certainly slow, ride through it.

It was a relatively small place with a performance area that couldn't handle large festivals or major music attractions, but in its color, verve, and something-new-around-every-corner surprises, it was a hit.

It attracted more people its first summer than all of the other Rock Island parks put together.

It attracted Bill Fleming occasionally at lunchtime, and every so often Roger Pice, who was now using the name of Francis Balch.

But it didn't attract Jane Tressel in her yellow shorts. That is, during the week it didn't. But sometimes on Saturdays or Sundays it did attract her – as least enough for a rest and a view of the water from a stop rather than movement.

Then she enjoyed the view so much that she didn't notice the two men who sometimes were both scoping her out.

Chapter 43

Duane – Watching Jane

Duane's heart rate leaped. But he was used to it, especially around 6:30 almost every evening when YB appeared. YB was Yellow Bird in his little note book. He somehow didn't want to write "Yellow Bird" down. First of all, it would mean a whole column of "Yellow Birds" down the pages of the cheap book, she appeared that often. And secondly, he felt a little squeamish about the word "bird." It would make him appear as, perhaps, one of those nature loving birdwatchers. What if someone – someone like Wilber – found the book? Duane would never hear the end of it. During the time when they switched shifts – perhaps 15 minutes when they were together – Wilber could be merciless. He had a nasty edge to him, jumping at almost every thing that Duane did that wasn't absolutely by the book.

One time the homeless guy – Duane called him "the sad sack" - fell off his log and rolled into the river during Duane's shift. When he told Wilber about it, with a knowing grin on his face, Wilber jumped at him: "Wadya mean? You were watching the shore? Watching an old bum? You're supposed to have your eyes on the trucks and the ledger – all the time, right? But you were a bum watcher. That's funny. Bum watcher. Duane. bum watcher."

For about two months after that Duane was "bum watcher" every time Wilber came to work.

Duane never said a word, just let it slide. Eventually Wilber stopped using it. But it did bother Duane very much. Wilber was a bastard sometimes.

Recently Duane had a short conversation with Wilber, enduring Wilber's mild sarcasm about the Chicago Cubs, who were Duane's favorite baseball team – although, to be true, he really wasn't that much of a fan. He watched them occasionally on TV when he was home when they played, but he never listened to them on the radio at work. It was against the rules of his job. No radio or other distraction; one had to concentrate on the job. Duane thought the rule was absurd, but went along with it. It didn't bother him enough to cause him to get up tight. He suspected the other employees at the office brought along some of these new, very compact radios – some of them small enough to be concealed in the ear – but he would have none of it. He didn't want to compromise his job anymore than he did now with his binoculars and his note book. That was enough. That and the fact of his glorious Yellow Bird.

If Wilber found out about Yellow Bird, Duane would have a real problem. He didn't know if he could take it. So he kept his notebook secret, taking it home every night with him, not even keeping it in his lunchbox, but in a shirt pocket of the t-shirt he always wore underneath a regular shirt.

But now YB was drifting down the path as she usually did. What a sight! Duane went a little bit crazy. His binoculars were up and focused, his elbows resting on the shelf under the window, the window open with the cooler air of late afternoon and so he could get a clear look as she passed. His mind went blank to almost everything else but her. The slough, the Arsenal across the water, his job, even the tiny office he was in – they all didn't exist. She was in focus and his focus – an image in crystal that was more real to him than any other aspect of his life.

He followed her as she swept upriver on the path. The yellow jersey tonight showed a perfect, to Duane, figure. She was gorgeous and in wonderful shape. Slim, curvaceous, and harmonious. An ideal goddess bicycling past him, now dipping down for a moment to go down a slight incline near the sewerage plant.

Wait a minute! What was that? Was that somebody's head? Duane caught himself. He wanted to continue following her with the glasses as he always did, keeping her in the middle of the glass until she was obscured by the trees which grew close to the slough's edge. But he stopped. He was sure he had seen a head, covered with a cap, behind her as she hit the level path.

He stopped watching her and reversed his sweep back to where he thought the head appeared. Nothing. Nothing was there. As he shifted the glasses back and forth and even down to the slough, he could see nothing out of the normal, certainly nothing like a person – no other biker, no walker, and nobody sitting along the shore of the water.

But Duane was sure he had seen a head, probably a man's, covered with a cap, looking out over the path watching the female rider. Why just a head? Was the person lying on the ground on the other side of the path? No, Yellow Bird possibly would have seem the person and reacted. Duane was sure that she had not seen the head; she hadn't faltered or shifted her cadence in any way.

Duane tried to remember the face on the head, but he couldn't. He drew a blank. He wasn't even sure it was male. He knew it was Caucasian, not black or brown, simply because of the coloring, but beyond that, nothing.

He was alarmed, but not overly so. After all, the head did nothing, just looked. Wasn't that what Duane did? Just looked and didn't act?

But tonight after he got off his shift he would act. He would act at least to the extent of looking around where he saw the head to see if he could find anything. But first he would keep a close watch when she returned to see if the head appeared again. Duane noted in this book: "6:34,YB, someone watched behind."

At 7:13 Yellow Bird appeared again, doing nothing out of the ordinary, going slightly slower into the moderate wind, but keeping a steady pace. This time she was going west, just as she did every time in the evening when she bicycled the path. Duane drew a bead on her with his binoculars, keeping her in the center of the glass, watching her perfect beauty and grace. But when she came just about opposite him, he diverted his eye to watching intently for anything behind her.

Nothing. No head. Nothing.

But later Duane did check the side of the path - after he had closed up for the evening, after he had walked downstairs – saying goodby to the night watchman in his cubicle next to the door. He was about to walk to the lot where his car was parked when he stopped and looked around. He could walk to the spot where he estimated the head had been. He would take a look? He walked down the trail but the different perspective made him not sure exactly where he had seen the fleeting head. He scrutinized the slough side of the trail, but he could see nothing out of the ordinary. Just the usual rubble, old tie wedges, and some debris blown in from the businesses along the slough.

He carefully eased himself down the embankment, stopping occasionally to try to discern just where he would be when someone's head would appear over the levee from the viewpoint of his office. Bingo! Almost all the way down the slope he knew he was in the right position, He could see the path and he was in a bee line to the office's window, now a tiny obscure opening. But nothing caught his eye as he looked around. He walked back and forth on the shore of the slough a few times, perhaps 20 yards in each direction, and that was that. Whoever had been there – if they indeed had been – had left no trace. Given the stony nature of the area, that was no surprise.

But as he turned to climb back up to the trail, he saw something – something beneath a large mallow weed with leaves extending out in all directions. It was a flash of yellow.

He kicked at the mallow and disclosed a water bottle, one similar to those used by bicyclists. He picked it up and saw that its color had faded and the screw-lid top somewhat cracked. It had some printing – a local bike shop's address and phone number.

It could have been dropped by anyone. But it was yellow, however faded, He tried to remember if she used a bottle like this, but only her face came up in his memory. Next time we would try to note the water bottle she used. For now, though, he kept the bottle and carried it to his home.

Chapter 44

Kids on Sylvan Island

It's kids' heaven.

Get this: a big teardrop of land, about 55 square acres, completely enclosed by water. Sure, it's an island, but only technically so, for the two streams of water which surround it are minimal rivers compared to the big daddy Mississippi broiling away a half mile to the north. This dollop of an island is really a scoop out of a bigger island in the Mississippi River. The main current – and most of the water – is in the distance, for all practical (and playful) purposes invisible.

This kids' heaven island isn't that isolated; it even has a bridge – a bridge with a big bolder of a concrete block right in the middle of its entrance where it connects to the mainland. And that, of course, means no cars, trucks, or other big lumbering machines.

Of course, if you take cars away, there go most people – grownups obviously. Very few self-respecting adults would deign to have to walk to get on an island. And once he or she got there, what's to see. No roads, no parking areas, no scenic lookouts, no reason to go, no way.

Oh, some nuts occasionally. Bird watchers, fishermen, homeless bums, compulsive walkers, lovers looking for privacy – and, of course, kids.

They love it. It's heaven.

It's a treasure island of adventure, a pirate's hiding place, a Huck Finn dream of "lighting out to the territory," a private Swiss Family Robinson, a temporary Lord of the Flies, a living-breathing video game of surprise and expectation.

Kids, mostly boys, go there and romp. Run around the many paths. Mountain bike up and down the kid-size ridges. Throw a line in and catch a catfish. Build a clubhouse with discarded planks, tree limbs, and big corrugated cartons. Play "hide and go seek." Play war. Play terrorist. Build fires. Drink pop. Smoke cigarettes. Look at dirty pictures. Get away from adults.

Teens, almost always boys, go there also. Swagger through the obscure trails. Mountain bike. Smoke pot. Drink beer. Play boom boxes. Intimidate little kids. Talk, scream, and yell. Raise hell, whatever that means. Have sex, or try to if a girl can be lured to the place. Smash things. Look at dirty pictures. Throw things. Burn things. Get away from adults.

One time, as the story goes, three bored teenager roasted a kid there. Nobody ever heard about it, and no one was punished, but the kid was held captive and almost literally grilled over an open fire. He ended up with some charred and smoky clothing, one shoe completely useless because of a melted sole, and having to make up an enormous lie to tell his less-than-attentive mother.

Billy Joe Snyder was a nasty kid anyway. The three teens knew it. They went to high school, but sometimes after school walked down to the island and hung out there until they got hungry or had something else to do. Mostly they had all kinds of free time, homework not being their particular bent. The three would occasionally see Billy Joe lording it over some kids he had brought with him or ran into at the island.

Usually Billy Joe got into shoving. That was his thing, the teens recognized. He didn't shout so much or pester or throw things. He shoved. Many times from behind. They'd see him with another kid his age, sometimes bigger, sometimes smaller. Size didn't matter. What mattered was that most of the time they would get into some conflict and Billy Joe would just get up and walk away. But he wouldn't go far. He'd disappear into the brush, but then stop and just watch the kid he had been talking to. When the kid would get bored and start walking somewhere, Billy Joe went into action. Whoosh, out of the woods, he would rush up behind the kid, give him a quick shove, and laugh heartily when the kid inevitably fell sprawling to the ground.

Let the punishment fit the crime, the teens figured. So they tried shoving. They did serial shoving – one right after the other. One after the other sneaking from behind and knocking the bully down, then sneaking back into the brush and waiting for another turn. Billy Joe took it OK, but usually he lammed out quickly before the message could be shoved into him.

So the teens tried something worse. On a sunny late afternoon, they saw the bully shoving a little kid, who they recognized as a boy who was interested in woodcarving – and pretty good at it. He sometimes showed them his work; he liked to turn driftwood into action figures that he saw on TV. The teens nicknamed him Captain Saturday because all his heroes were from Saturday morning TV. He never painted his creations, just showed them around and then burned them on the outside. He had a whole collection of little four-inch figure, each a smudged black, burnished shinny by constant friction with his clothes, his book bag, or his clever little hands.

The day in question Billy Joe not only shoved Captain Saturday unusually hard, knocking him on his back with a sudden jerk, but he grabbed the Captain's bag and jumped on it, smashing whatever was in, presumably the boy's precious collection of carvings.

That was too much. Soon Billy Joe was trussed up, gagged and being pushed around a small campfire that the teens started with some weeds, cardboard, and a few rotten tree branches.

"You punk bastard, we're gonna grill you and burn you so you're just like one of those black heroes that was in the bag."

Billy Joe tried to mumble something, but the gag – one old sock stuffed into his mouth and the other sock tied around his head - worked. Nothing intelligible came out.

"You grab his legs and I'll get his shoulders and let's put him on the grill." The boys did it, lifting Billy Joe into the air horizontally.

Now the sounds coming from the gag were intelligible – yells of anguish and apprehension, accompanied by squirming and contorted body movements in an attempt to get away. It didn't work though. The teens gripped him securely and raised him so he was above the fire.

"Hey, throw some weeds on the fire; let's have some smoke."

Soon Billy Joe was immersed in smelly white smoke, breathing and coughing in convulsions, twisting and spiraling in a futile attempt to get away from the smoke and the heat.

Then the teens grabbed his body and upper legs and positioned his feet above the fire, slowly moving them closer and closer. It wasn't long before smoke was also coming from the soles of Billy Joe's shoes, and he was convulsively twisting and jerking – anything to avoid the heat.

"Wadda you think? Should we take off those shoes and make everything black, just like those little wood guys that you just stomped on?"

Billy Joe showed that he heard with a tremendous lurch of his lower body, but it wasn't enough to make the three teens lose their grips. One of them did, however, grab the rag that was acting as the gag and yanked it away.

Billy Joe was bawling uncontrollably. "Yeolllllll! I give! I give! My feet. My feet are burning. Yoellll!"

"OK, Billy Joe, it's your call. You gonna give up the shoving or are you gonna walk around on blackened stubs where your feet were?"

"Shoving? Shoving? What do you mean, shoving? You mean pushing those kids around?

"Yeah, either shoving or stubs, you make the call."

"Owah. OK, OK, I give up. No more shoving or pushing or whatever. I promise. Just let me up. Get me away from this fire."

Billy Joe limped home that afternoon. When his mother asked him why he smelled of smoke so strongly, he replied, "Some guys had a fire, out to Sylvan, and we were goofing around it. I guess I got too close to it. Yea, too close."

"Billy Joe, what's this? What did you do to your shoes? They're black."

"Oh that. Well, I had my shoes off and I guess that ol' Jacko accidentally kicked them into the fire for awhile. But I got them out in time, didn't I? They're not too bad, not too . . ."

Billy Joe hardly ever showed up at Sylvan Island after that. If someone asked him why, he would reply, "Oh, ol' Sylvan, I got better things to do. That's a kids' place anyway."

He was right in one respect. Sylvan Island was a kids' place – more than a place, it was a real kids' heaven.

Chapter 45

Jane Rides with the Club

It gnawed in the back of her mind for about a week. Why shouldn't she go for a ride with the bicycle club? She was no shrinking violet, afraid to meet with a group of strangers and go for a ride with them, even if they didn't know her and probably would associate with their own riding friends.

Plus she was getting somewhat bored with basically the same biking geography almost every day. She loved the trail, especially the section along Sylvan Slough, but she could use a little novelty in her bicycling.

And then there was the daunting glitz in her mind of the possibility of a stalker. Getting away for a ride outside her normal haunts with a new group of people might clear her mind of the cobwebs of hesitation and apprehension.

So one evening – with her husband absent, as usual of late - she went to Google and soon found the web site for the Quad Cities Bicycle Club. It was an impressive site, not something thrown together from a template from no-cost software. No the site had all the bells and whistles that the big boys had, the sites sponsored by companies with money, or non-profits with contributors with tax write-off donations.

When she clicked on the calendar icon, a long list of the club's bike rides scrolled into view.

One of the rides was for the Saturday morning just two days away. That would work. She had nothing else in view. And it started in Illinois, at the border between Moline and East Moline. That also would work for her. She wouldn't even have to use her car to get there. The ride's mileage was listed as 45 miles. Even with the added miles to get to it, she was confident she could handle it.

So why not do it?

And that Saturday morning at about 7:30, leaving her husband twisting and turning in bed, she was on the path along Sylvan Slough heading east to the beginning of the club ride. Just as she got to the point where the lines of water from the two dams come together, wouldn't you know it, she noticed a rider following her. But he wasn't stalking her; he was coming fast, gaining ground on her.

When he got close, she noticed in her mirror that he was the same man who had talked to her before about the bike club and its rides.

He yelled at her from behind. "Where the hell you going so fast? I'm all sweated up already just trying to get around you."

She swerved her head momentarily to see just who it was. "Oh, it's you, the guy I accused of sta . . . following me."

He came up to the left side of her. "You know, it's getting to the point that we must own this path. It seems to be just you and me all the time."

"What do you do, wait for me to come down the hill and then take off after me?"

"Well, sure. Most of the time I spend the entire night just sitting on my bike waiting – and waiting. Waiting for the sun and your yellow jersey."

"I'll bet."

"Actually I was running late this morning. Had to gulp down my Grape-nuts. I'm going on the club ride up at the other end of Moline – that's where it starts."

"Hey, guess what? I'm going to the same thing. I listened to what you said the other day when we talked and I checked around and found out about the ride this morning. So why not. I'm on it."

"You're going to it. Hey, we can ride to it together. I'm Bill, by the way."

"And I'm Jane. Jane Tressel.

By this time they were on the section of the path called the Butterworth Trail. It is not the best for two riders holding a conversation since it is somewhat narrow and usually has lots of traffic. It is without a doubt the most popular trail in the Quad Cities, beating out Davenport's downtown one, and both the Rock Island one to the west and the East Moline one to the east. It's popularity comes from its wide open views of the river and its nicely manicured grounds and resting places. It even has some restroom facilities, something lacking in most of the other riverfront paths.

But now before 8 o'clock in the morning the path wasn't busy enough to prevent the two of them from talking back and forth and – what it amounted to – finding out about each other.

Coming upon the big parking lot at the border, their destination, it was obvious even to Jane that a group ride was going to take place. Bikes and cars with back racks commandeered the parking lot. People in a dazzling variety of jerseys were either adjusting their bikes, milling around, or just patiently waiting in a broad oval around a bike rider who seemed to be in charge.

Bill had a glancing acquaintance with a few of the riders, but no real friends or major riding buddies. As it turned out – from what they learned about each other as they rode now north on the trail – they were both somewhat solitary riders. They didn't ride much during the major parts of the day, hardly ever in the afternoon. They always had other things to do. But the early mornings were different. They both loved to ride with the emerging sun.

The ride went out to some of the county roads for some low-traffic mileage before converging to the trail at the village of Albany where a couple of good restaurants featured breakfasts up until 11:00. Breakfast or lunch; they were both hungry.

Bill had an order of stuffed French toast with grilled sausage on the side and Jane opted for a Spanish omelet. The bikers pushed a number of tables together to become a biking breakfast party. It was fun. Lots of bike talk before the chatter was diminished with the arrival of the waitress's big tray of breakfast plates.

As the two of them were mounting their bikes, ready to take the path directly south to their respective homes, Bill remarked, "This is quite an international ride, don't you know."

Jane didn't get it. "International. Hmm. Seemed like Midwest to me."

"What do you mean: French toast, Spanish omelet, and you know what my last name is? Fleming. And that's pretty close to Flemish. Very European."

Needless to say, they both had a good time. And no stalker was up and about.

Chapter 46

Bill – a Step Up

His bike stashed in a basement storage room, Bill was at his desk promptly at 8:30. He had a half hour to get things set up for the day, make preliminary notes about appointments coming up, and just in general make sure everything in his sphere of responsibility was running smoothly.

As he looked through his notes, the entry about the seemingly homeless man – Francis Balch - came up. Bill was a little apprehensive still about the man and his savings account and safe deposit box. But in the weeks since he had appeared, no untoward happenings occurred with him. In fact Bill did notice that when the man appeared at the bank he was looking incrementally more presentable. But still the name did not fit right: Francis Balch. However, he had the proper credentials, and Bill had copies of them.

About ten minutes before the bank's opening time of nine, his immediate supervisor, Melba Stonebark, stopped at his desk. She was a pleasant woman, middle aged and nicely groomed except for her teeth. They were not aligned correctly, one askew, right in front, seeming to be creeping between the two teeth surrounding it. But her teeth were no matter; he got along with her well. She hardly ever corrected his work and he didn't hesitate to take problems to her when he was in doubt.

With a wide open – even toothy - smile, she said, "Good morning, Bill. Hey, I'm glad you're sitting down because I have some news for you."

Bill became a little apprehensive. What possible news could she have? "Oh, hit me now before I get bogged down with these debit accounts and lose track of what's important."

"The good news is that you're being promoted."

"Promoted? What? Hey I haven't been here that long. Promoted to what? Do I get to mop up the place after work on weekends, or what?"

"Oh, come on, Bill. You're always joking around. Be serious now."

"Serious? How do you spell that? With a "uo" or a "ou"?"

She brightened, "You spell is with an "OP." as in Operations Manager. What do you think of that spelling?"

"Wait a minute. Operations Manager? Are you serious?"

"We had a meeting yesterday afternoon – late. We went over all the

134

prospects, and – guess what – you turned out to be the best. You've done a top-notch job since you've been here, and we – that's all the other officers – think you can handle the job when Sam Yuma retires, and that's just a matter of weeks."

"Let me get this straight. All of you want me to be a bank officer, the office manager. Wow, I'm glad I'm sitting down."

"Well, Bill, what do you think. Will you accept the position?"

"You'll have to give me some time to think about it. Let me go out on my bike – no, I don't need to go outside. I'll just make a quick loop around the basement parking lot . . . Ah, come on Melba, you know the answer. Yes, yes, yes."

All that morning Bill was in shock, but in a happy, almost delirious shock. He was going to be a bank officer in his hometown bank. He could hardly believe it.

The word got out among the other employees of the bank. The tellers almost to a person made it a point to congratulate him. Even Frank Daniels and Gloria Sheely, mid-level administrators, gave him a smile and a hand shake, even though they realized that they had been passed over for the position. But they both liked Bill and knew that they could work closely with him.

About 11 o'clock Francis Balch shuffled through the revolving door of the main entrance. He was wearing what appeared to be a new shirt, at least it was clean, not stained. But he had on the same pants that he always wore, grass stained though they be. One side of the pants seemed to Bill to be lower than the other, as if some extra weight was in the pocket on that side.

Francis gave a slight smile to Bill, acknowledging Bill's extraordinary smile. He walked past Bill's desk, which was near the main passageway, but he didn't say anything. He just kept on going, heading towards the entrance to the safe deposit boxes.

But as Bill watched him disappear down the beautifully tiled passageway, his smile turned to chagrin.

Francis was wearing a new pair of shoes – a new pair of Moc-a-Step shoes.

Chapter 47

Roger - Coins in the bank

Roger was sitting in his little apartment and in his mind he was sitting pretty – feeling better than he had ever felt in his entire life. He wasn't homeless, for one thing, even if his home was a rather shabby one room apartment. But it wasn't a cot in a homeless shelter, a niche in the concrete below a bridge, a corrugated box in an out-of-the-way place in a public park, or – perhaps the worse – a dank and muddy "cave" in the embankment of an offshoot of the Mississippi River.

He had some decent clothes. One thing he learned while being homeless is that used clothes were easy to come by, if you didn't mind them being somewhat worn and out of style. Many churches and agencies accepted donations of clothes – many of them from the families of recently deceased people – and they gave them out regularly to anyone who would accept them. The back rooms of church basements were stuffed with old clothes.

Just recently while biking down to the river he stopped at the Apostolic Church of the Holy Eternity when he saw a sign announcing a clothing giveaway taking place right then. Why not? He stopped. In the basement he selected a beautiful green and blue sport shirt, clean and almost looking new. He picked up a used pair of blue jeans, just his size. But the crowning touch took place when he passed the table covered with shoes. There right in the center was a pair of Moc-a-Step shoes, looking as new as the day they came out of the box. He grabbed them and checked out the size. Ah, 11. He normally wore a 10 or 10 1/2, something like that. He found a chair and tried them on. A little bit big, but what's not to like. Moc-a-Steps and almost new.

As he was saying thanks to the two gray haired ladies in charge, in the back of his mind he wondered why someone would give away such a nice pair of shoes. He couldn't comprehend it, but then there were many things that he couldn't comprehend.

The major change, however, in his life was the fact that he now had money. Never in his life had he ever had more than a hundred dollars at one time. Now he had thousands of dollars – some in a savings account, some stashed away in a safe deposit box, and some in his pocket right now.

The money almost seemed to alleviate the gnawing turmoil of his previous life – a life overwhelmed by the death of his childhood friend. If it didn't take away the concern completely, it certainly eased the pain.

But he - now in a much more conscious frame of mind, one that was slowly becoming aware of the usual life around him – had acquired another gnawing, if not fear, at least anxiety.

It was the money – those 20 dollar gold coins still buried in the muddy side of Sylvan Slough. He had to get them out and put them in the safe deposit box. Why hadn't he done that before? In his mind, the answer wasn't clear. But it was becoming more clear with every day.

The next morning after a dinner the night before of hamburgers fried on his little frying pan and some French fries heated in the same pan he biked down to his cave. Finding the place where he had buried the coins, he wrapped them in one of the socks that he had taken from the clothes giveaway.

He waited until mid-morning before going to the bank. As he strode through the lobby, he was proud of himself. He was wearing a clean shirt, was relatively clean shaven, and – the crowning touch – was wearing his new pair of Moc-a-step shoes.

Wouldn't the man – he thought his name was Bill something or other – who had signed him up at the bank be proud of him!

Chapter 48

Roger – Jane's Picture

The hatch marks so thick in the mist that hovered around Roger's memory were easing, spreading themselves, becoming more and more transparent the more he lived as an independent human being rather than an independent homeless bum.

Those gold coins – the golden treasure that the river deposited in his lap – now safely held within the posts and pillars of the bank vault were, nevertheless, increasingly popping up in his consciousness. What were they really worth? Was the maternal lady at the coin company doing him justice or was he being taken as he had been so many times in his life?

The library was the answer and with it another clearing of the wisps in his memory. His stint at the Acorn Institute, working in the office, taking care of many of the routine details of a large institution, came back to him. He remembered that he enjoyed the basic clerking work that kindly Mrs. Lofter let him do. He became good at it – if he concentrated. But then his concentration could be broken easily. Sometimes just a gurgle of flowing water put him into an involuntary trance.

But now at the Rock Island Public Library with its large bank of computers just to the right of the main entrance he slipped back into the mindset – the office mode – that he remembered from the California Institute.

He asked the bushy-haired, middle aged lady behind the desk overlooking the computers how he could find out about coin collecting and the latest prices for old coins. It didn't take her long to have him with both a library card – his ID was from California, but he showed her a receipt for the rental of his room – and a basic familiarity with how to use the library computers. Even his long dormant basic computer skills came back with the white-faced lady's guidance.

Within fifteen minutes he secretly had one of his coins in his hand and was comparing it to the illustration on his computer's monitor. Ebay listed the identical coin, not even in the best of condition, as worth $2,550 as a starting point. With his 36 coins we was wealthy. He sat back in the chair, replaced his coin securely in his money belt which he had picked up for almost nothing at the resale store near the path in Rock Island, and with a quick mental calculation realized that he had enough money to live without working for years and years. To him, he was set forever.

Of course, he had to keep his wealth safe. He knew what it was like to live in the underworld of the homeless, the jobless, and the morality- less. He had to be extremely careful about taking care of his coins. He couldn't show them to anyone – except the woman at the coin shop over in Davenport who bought the one from him.

He was assured, but not completely so, with the safe deposit box, outwardly so impressive, that the man at the bank set him up with. But for now it was the best security that he could think of. Over the course of a number of weeks he had transferred all the coins to the vault – usually just a few at a time, in case he was robbed. And he was extremely wary of being observed going to the cache of coins in the embankment.

But he thought he had gotten away with it. Thousands of dollars of value owned by him now was safely locked up, and he had access and the right to take the coins out one at a time and turn them into dollars.

He sat back at the computer station and slightly relaxed. He had been up-tight when looking at the coins on the monitor, since library patrons around him could easily observe what he was looking at. But no one appeared to be interested, all perusing with intensity the web sites they were studying.

Just to the right and ahead of him in the next row, he suddenly noticed the head of hair of the woman at the computer. It was a very pleasing black and styled in a modern way, or so Roger thought. He most assuredly was not "up" on the latest styles.

Could the woman be the same woman he had observed on the path so many times, biking past him in a yellow jersey?

What would she be doing here – she seemed to be above using a public facility for computer work. She would have her own computer – or had access to one owned by a company – he was sure.

She turned her head to take a look at the notebook to her left and he knew immediately she wasn't the woman he was thinking of. This woman's cheeks were puffy, almost closing up her eyes.

Still something about the hair and the back of the woman's head caused another leap in his memory. A flickering image of his sister, Jane, momentarily appeared, but not as she normally was in the few times he struggled to remember her. His memory pictured her wearing an old-fashioned dress – long skirt and frilly sleeves.

Then he remembered. She had been in a play at the high school, and they had put a picture of her and one of the actors in the newspaper before the drama was performed. "Our Town" sped to his consciousness. Yes, that was the name of the play. And he even remembered that she had the part of Emily. He remembered her in the play's last scene: she just sitting plainly on a chair with others from the cast, gazing off in the distance as if they were dead – which they were supposed to be.

He would really like to see that picture again. In his mind that image of his sister was remarkably like the image of the woman on the bike who flashed by him so many times.

So why not? He started by Googling "Jane Pice." Of the three entries that came up, none were even remotely close to what he imagined her life to be. He had been out of touch with his family and his sister. What if she were married and now had a different name? He then tried the search engine on "Our Town," Rock Island High School. After a long search he was soon scrolling through a series of articles about the play. But there was nothing about his high school's long ago production.

Then, boom! There the article was – and, best of all, a picture accompanied it. It was in black and white and not as clear as modern photos, but immediately he knew that it was his sister in the picture.

He stared at it for a long time, memorizing its details and trying to force his mind to bring back what she looked like in real life when he was a youngster.

The more he stared at it, the more it morphed into the image in his mind of the lady on the path.

What if, indeed, she was his sister, Jane?

He got up and asked the reference librarian if it was possible to make a copy of what was on the screen. He could – for a slight fee. He eagerly paid it and soon had a copy of his long forgotten sister as she was back before his terrible turmoil. He folded the copy carefully and slipped it into the front left pocket of his jeans.

As he left the library, he was eager to go to the path and hopefully see the woman in yellow – and see if she could possibly be his sister.

But that was not to be happen this day.

He biked down the path along Sylvan Slough, but as he was going past where his cave – and his coin storage - had been, he was literally knocked off his bike by two men. They jumped on him, held him down, and rapidly searched his pockets.

One of them, thin and with a tattoo of a chain running around the left side of his neck, hissed in his ear: "Where is it? We know you got something."

His buddy, who for some reason had on two different shoes, one brown and one an off shade of beige, said, "He ain't go nottin'. Just a couple of fives rolled up in his pocket. Shit, the way he's been sneakin' around here, I figured he would have something worth something."

The tattoo said, "You're right. Nothing. Two fives, some change, and – what's this? Just a piece of paper with an old picture on it. Some girl in an old fashioned dress." He crumbled up the paper and tossed it aside where it lodged next to a fledgling tree. "OK, buddy, where's your money? Where've you got it hidden?"

Roger was about to say something, to tell them he didn't have anything, when the tattoo man interrupted.

"Aw aw, here comes someone on a bike. Let's give this guy a shove and get out of here."

With the punch Roger rolled down the slope about three feet where he curled up into a fetal position, hoping not to be beaten up. But the two assailants took off.

Within a few seconds, Jane came rolling by, momentarily noticing the bum who seemed to be sleeping on the side of the path, but not recognizing him. She pondered telling one of her policeman friends about it, but since this was the first bum sighting in a long time, she decided not to do anything about it right now.

Roger, his eyes closed and his face lodged in the crook of his arm, did not see her go by.

He also did not notice the crumbled-up paper lying almost next to him on the side of the slough.

Chapter 49

Bobby - the picture

Skateboarding down the path, Bobby Scott was somewhat troubled. Things had not been going well at school. Ms Bennet, his computer graphics teacher, had conned him into helping some kids who weren't doing very well after he had completed each day's class work. Oh, it was OK, even if two of the three were real losers who spent most of their time in the class just goofing around and sending almost obscene tweets to each other. But one, a recently arrived immigrant from Africa, was intently interested in making sense out of the computer work, but was woefully lacking in background. He had never had access to a compute before and hardly knew the basics of it. Bobby spent most of his free class time with him.

But Bobby didn't like to give up the time on the computer and its fairly advanced graphic software. And it also took him away from his desk and his chances to get into conversation with Marie. The more he talked to her, the more he liked her. And he thought that she somehow enjoyed talking to him also. Now, with the tutoring, he didn't have the five minutes or so with her at the end of class. But he liked Ms Bennet so much that he couldn't refuse her – and she did have a big job keeping her big class on task.

But now, coming down a slight incline along Sylvan Slough, he saw a man lying scrunched-up in the bramble along the the path. Actually all he saw was the back of the man, his shirt and pants indistinguishable and somewhat dirty. When Bobby slowed down, the man let out a moan.

Bobby stopped and took a long look at the man rolled almost into a ball. He recognized him, thought he had seen him along the path in the past. Then the man moved, straightened up somewhat, and moaned again.

Bobby, against his better judgment, went to the man and touched him on the back of his shoulder.

"Hey, man, are you all right?"

All that came out was a another moan.

"What'd you do, fall?"

Then the man, who was Roger, pushed himself up by his arms and slowly got to his feet. He was unharmed, but somewhat bewildered. He said to the young boy: "I'm OK, damn it. Get away. I don't need you. Get away."

"Hey, man, I was just trying to help, that's all."

Roger's hands moved to his pockets. He pulled them out, one by one. Nothing. Each pocket was empty. He let them hang along the sides of his pants. "See, nothing. I ain't got nothing."

"That's all right, old man, I don't want anything. I'm just trying to help out. Are you OK? Are you hurt?"

Roger didn't even say anything, just looked at Bobby closely and then turned to the side of the path and started walking away. "I'm OK. I just had . . . I'm OK." He walked in the opposite direction that Bobby had been skating, walked to an old bike lying on the opposite side of the path.

Bobby watched him go and then remembered him from Schwiebert Park, sitting on a bench just watching the river and the people in the area. Now he was gone, walking away to the bike and mounting it.

He was gone and Bobby just stood there, watching.

Then he noticed something in the gravel very close to where the man had been lying. It was a crumpled-up piece of paper. It looked new, not weather beaten from rain or anything. Bobby picked it up and saw the paper's image – a high school aged girl in an old fashioned dress staring at the camera with a young man next to her.

The girl could have been Marie – or was it the woman in yellow? He couldn't tell. All he knew was that he knew the person in the picture. He was sure of that.

And after he had taken the picture to school, made a copy of it, enlarged it, downloaded it to his computer, and spent three days adding black, curly hair to it, he knew who the person in the picture was.

It was the bicycle rider in the yellow jersey.

Chapter 50

Jane – at Bill's Bank

Jane hadn't been to the First Security Bank for years, even though it was in downtown Rock Island where her ad agency was located. Her company used BlackHawk Savings and Trust, and her personal bank was one of the new ones closer to her home. But today she had a special interest in going to the signature bank in Rock Island.

The usual ad sales captain, Sally O'Kief, had had a hip replacement a week ago and was still not up to coming in and working. Jane didn't think any of Sally's underlings were quite ready enough for the job of getting the Rock Island giant to switch to their agency – at least for their local ads.

So she - wearing a light blue, crisply tailored suit with a white blouse and a subdued red scarf - and a promising young spitfire, Marla Bloom, just out of college, were going to see what they could do. They had an appointment with the bank's executive manager, Jody Schook, for 10 a.m. and were a bit early as they walked in the front door of the imposing, neoclassical building, and started down the marble floored main aisle with desks on each side, surrounded by more formal, book lined offices for the bank's management team.

Jane was always somewhat in awe at the luxuriance splendor of the place, built at a time when downtown Rock Island was the primary business and commercial center for not only the city, but also much of the surrounding cities and towns. The city's expansion to the south and the mall and big box explosion along the Rock River has left the downtown a somewhat bedraggled place of small businesses, old-line offices, and an ill considered attempt to turn the space into an entertainment area. The entertainment turned out to be drinking in the late weekend hours, with the resultant inebriated violence associated with it.

She and Marla stopped at a desk, commandeered by a young woman with long, dangling earrings glaring at a computer screen. As Jane told the woman that they had an appointment with the manager, Jody Schook, something caught her eye in an office behind the woman at the desk.

The something turned out to be Bill.

Jane was taken aback. It was Bill in an executive office. He was a higher-up in the management of this bank. She was somewhat abashed.

She and Bill had been occasionally riding together for a few weeks now, but it was not by form or prearrangement. They would meet because they liked the same times, the same routes, and the same emphasis to keep the mild fitness exercise that they enjoyed.

They had both ridden on club rides a few times, but again it was more by accident than by deliberate intention. On the last club ride – this one starting in Iowa – Bill had not appeared and she had ridden with three women who were friendly enough but not very interesting. But she had enjoyed herself. The rides were an expansion of her experiences and she enjoyed the wide open country that they occasionally rode through.

But here was the somewhat bashful – at least in her opinion - Bill in an executive office at the First Security Bank.

The Miss Earrings at the desk directed them to some chairs in front of a corner office and asked them to wait a few minutes; Jody Schook was on a conference call but would be finished very soon.

Jane glanced at the office where Bill sat behind a desk intently reading some papers with a pen hovering over them. He looked good – in the right place. Yes, he fit. They had never exchanged job stories – or much personal information, for that matter. For all she knew, he didn't even know if she were married or not, although she did wear a wedding ring. He did not. But she knew that some married men didn't go for the ring thing.

But still with just that quick glance, she felt herself redden a bit, felt a quickening, a tiny flutter – more than just recognition or friendship. She caught herself before her companion, Marla, could notice. She forced herself into her professional working mode.

Bill looked up and stared out his office door. His face was a blank, but then it brightened up like a cardinal amid a feeder of starlings. He dropped his pen on the desk and hurried over to her.

"Jane. I . . . I don't know what to say. Blue. I didn't recognize you."

"I haven't been in this bank for a long time. We bank elsewhere. But we'd like . . ."

Bill interrupted, "It's blue, not yellow. That's it. Hey, did you bike here? My bike is right downstairs. Let's go."

"No, no. I'm here on business. I'm meeting with – who is it, Marla – oh, yeah, Jody Schook."

Just then the woman with the earrings came up to then and led Jane and Marla into the adjacent office. But not before Bill, on an impulse, grabbed her hand and almost whispered, "After work. I'm ready for a nice ride."

That was all, but Jane was unsettled for the rest of the day – even though the meeting with the bank's executive manager had gone well. The manager, Jody, had even expressed some dissatisfaction with the ad agency they were presently using. She didn't mention that the new managing director, Bill Fleming, had told her that in his opinion, the campaign - "Local owned for local loans" was not getting much word of mouth usage.

When she had left the meeting and passed Bill's office, she slipped in quickly and nonchalantly laid her business card on his desk. He was on the phone, so she just smiled and left.

Chapter 51

Bill - Jane on his Mind

Jane's business card was perched on a shelf right above Bill's home computer. He had, of course, put all the pertinent data into the bank's computer system. But, here at home, he had gone further. Through the internet and some of the bank's proprietary software, he had learned much about her. He knew she was a "executive enhancement representative" for the Haver, Osborne, and Teakon ad agency, that she was very active in organizing cooperative events for the ad agencies of the area, that she was married to Fred Tressel who had a position at an auto parts branch of NAPA, that she and her husband owned their home, that she drove a Honda Insight, and that her driving record was exemplary.

In short, she was a real find.

To Bill, she was an ideal – an upwardly mobile, upper level ad agency operative who was also beautiful. She was a good biker who took her biking seriously, but not at a maniacal level. She also seemed to enjoy his company on the occasional times that accident put them together.

To Bill she had one problem, however, She was married.

He checked out her husband, Fred, but didn't find much above the basics. He seemed to be undistinguished and in a somewhat lackluster job. Bill could never remember meeting him or seeing another man riding with Jane. Evidently her husband was not into biking. But that was not that unusual. Many couples had differing interests in off-the-job pursuits.

But Bill did nothing with the information he had gathered. He was interested, but more curious than anything, after all, she was - for all he knew - happily married and just a person who was friendly to him.

He did take one action, however, that perhaps subconsciously led him to be closer to Jane. He made a point at the next weekly management meeting to rather forcefully complain about the ineffectiveness of the bank's local advertising campaign and the less than enthusiastic responses from the agency's staff responsible for it.

He showed his managers a graph that he had compiled of the increase in viable loans in the last two months and it had shown that rather than an increase, loans had actually decreased compared to the previous year at the same time. He had tried to set up a meeting with the agency, but he had not heard from them yet. He would try again, but perhaps this might be the time to start thinking of making a change to a different agency.

It worked. Bill's boss, Jody Schook, told him to search around discretely for a possible change. She mentioned that she had been visited recently by two representatives from an agency right here in downtown Rock Island, and was very impressed.

Two days later Bill found himself at Bennigan's enjoying a business lunch with Jane and Sally O'Kief, her agency's top salesperson. The meeting was very successful – lots of light banter, a serious discussion of the problems with working in the downtown, and a clarification of the various amenities the agency would offer the bank, besides an innovative new local advertising campaign.

Bill asked the two women to email him specific details about a package for the bank, along with typical pricing parameters. He also set up an appointment for him to tour their ad agency.

Bill was hyped.

Jane was not only beautiful, but she was very intelligent, with a wonderful command of the entire scope of not only her job, but the larger agency as well.

All that afternoon he was in a slightly nervous, anticipatory condition. It wasn't the possibility of his leadership in changing the bank's local ad campaign, it was the possibility that he would see Jane on the path that evening.

But he didn't see her. And he did see – but felt – something strange going on around him. For one thing, the serenely crystal air over the river to the west of the tip of Arsenal Island changed as he pedaled up the Sylvan Slough path. The air became heavy, slightly more oppressive with each minute of his travel. The sky darkened by degrees, with none of the rolling clouds so obvious just a while back along the main river.

The other strange thing was the feeling – not confirmed by sight – that he was being followed - if not followed, but somehow being observed. Why it popped into his mind, he had no answer. Even thought Jane had complained about feeling someone was stalking her, Bill had never had that feeling , not even an inkling.

Now he had.

He cruised along the path to the Rock Island/Moline border, where the entrance to Sylvan Island lay. Even though it was darkening, he – on a whim, or was it something more substantial? - made a turn and took the bridge over to the island. He took a left at a grassy path and followed it to the island's tip – a shore of dirt, small pebbles and a few big boulders.The setting sun suddenly broke through the overcast clouds. Bill looked up, squinting. A flicker of movement seemed to pass overhead. The light was so blinding that he could not be sure of what it was.

But it sounded like wings to him – large wings.

Chapter 52

Jane – the Kiss

They were on a Sunday morning club ride which started where they normally parked their cars, if they drove to the starting place. Bill didn't drive; he made it a point to bike to a bike ride.

Bill arrived a full 15 minutes before the scheduled 8 a.m. start of the ride, and there she was taking her bike off the rack on her car. They had not planned to ride this ride together, but as they looked around and didn't see anyone of close friendship to either of them, they just naturally set out side by side, talking when they had a chance.

They sat next to each other at the Albany Cafe where most of the riders assembled for the obligatory late breakfast of either pancakes, waffles, or the specialty of Gene, the fry cook, stuffed French toast.

On the way back – not on the Mississippi River Great River Trail, but on a series of country roads to the east of the river – they became separated from the few riders who were close to them, and it started to rain.

Wanting to stop and put his rain jacket on, Bill pulled off the road at the next intersection, a gravel road which boasted a ramshackle hut near it. It evidently has been built to act as a fresh vegetable and fruit farmer's stop, but it was sadly out of sorts. It, however, did have a projecting short roof along one side. He yelled to Jane: "Come on over here. It won't last long. We can stand under this little bit of shelter – provided it doesn't fall in on us."

There they stood, their bikes getting somewhat drenched, but they comparatively dry, especially since the wind was blowing directly behind the little hut.

Their chatting back and forth continued almost as if they were still on bikes, but eventually it faded into both of them staring out at the country road, not saying anything – just staring.

The rain came down with a surge, spattering along the edge of the hut, turning into a mist that enveloped them both. Bill edged close to her with his back to the road, using his body to protect her from the deluge of water.

She didn't say a thing, just stared at the lightning bolt printed on the top of his jersey. Suddenly the rain let up. She raised her head and stared into his face.

And then abruptly, she leaned into him and gave him a kiss – unexpected and involuntary. But it wasn't just a peck. Her lips lingered for more than a moment on his.

Then she eased back, smiled, and said, "Thanks for being such a comfort."

With that she was mounting her bike, the rain easing to a mere spattering of left-over drops.

"Come on, Bill, let's go. I needed your comfort, but now I need to get on my bike and make tracks."

They left, both happily roaring down the wet road, side by side, she contemplative, but he with a big grin on his face.

Chapter 53

Bill and Jane - on Sylvan Island

Bill and Jane met on a wonderful early July summer evening – the skies to the west a phantasmagoria of multi-swirls of color. From a premonition, or just an inkling, he was at the parking lot when she pulled in. He rushed to her car and started unfastening the stays holding her bike to its rack.

"Guess what, Jane?"

"You're going to move in with the homeless guys under the bridge?"

"Nope, nothing so normal as that. It's just that . . ." here he stopped, held his breath, let out a great puff of wind and said, "We're going with HOT – yep, your agency, the hot one.".

It took her only a half a second to erupt, springing to him as he cradled her bike in his arms, crushing the bike to both of them, her arms gripping his shoulders, her face just inches away from his. "Oh, Bill, that's wonderful. Oh, I'm so happy. What happened? Tell me what happened."

"Well we were all in Jody's office and I had this loaded bow and arrow. I said, 'No one leaves until we go with Haver, Osborne, and Teakon. No one left and I didn't have to waste an arrow."

"Ah, come on, Bill. The truth."

"The truth is that on my first major proposal to the board, they fell for it hook, line, and stinky toes. But it was a shoe in – not the stinky toes – but going with you guys. We needed a new ad campaign, and yours was the most appealing. Plus your outline of support was outstanding – so much more than we have been getting."

Jane stepped back and just stood, an appealing smile on her face as she stared at Bill. This guy was something else.

Soon they were pedaling past Schwiebert Park, undulating slightly up and down in front of the pumping station building, passing the Botanical Center, and entering the path next to Sylvan Slough. Here they picked up a little speed, but not much because on a fine summer day such as this had been, the path held more users than usual. As they rode, the light, however, became gloomy, the sun obscured behind a mounting bank of dark clouds.

They passed a young man on a skateboard, all by himself, and staring at them with his head cocked as they approached him.

They passed a big guy on a shabby bike who hardly noticed their presence, intent as he seemed to be with looking on both sides of he path as if anticipating something.

When they came to the old wagon bridge which was the entrance to Sylvan Island, Bill called a halt.

"Hey, let's go on the island. I want to show you something before it gets too dark to see it."

With that they wheeled across the rusty old bridge, stopping on the other side where three paths took off in different directions. Bill pointed to the one to the left, and, although it was a dirt trail, it was used enough that it wasn't hard to bike over it.

Chapter 54

Bill and Jane – Bedlam

Soon the two of them, with their bikes on the ground, were sitting on the smooth river stone in the somewhat camouflaged brush enclosure.

Bill looked at her hard and said, "We just about missed it. I wanted to show you the view from here before the sunset, but it looks like the clouds got there before we got here."

Darkness was increasingly. But it was a mysterious darkness. It wasn't just the light; a stuffiness of atmosphere, suffused with an underlying muskiness covered the area.

With some hesitation, Bill said, "Actually, that's a lie – although, sure, I was hoping the sunset would be amazing. But the real reason I brought you here was this." With that he leaned forward and kissed her lightly on the lips. She responded with a slight increase of pressure. Soon his arms were around her back as he drew her in tightly. The kiss became ardent on both sides. Jane could feel her upper body, and especially her face, breaking out with minute beads of sweat and she knew her face was becoming flushed with pink.

Suddenly a blinding flash of white light broke them apart. The sky opened in front of them as with a great boom the dark clouds parted, revealing the sun, just above the horizon, at full blaze into their eyes. The boom was followed by an engulfing swishing noise, not steady, but alternating in volume from deafening to almost nothing.

Startled, they leapt to their feet.

"What the," almost yelled Bill. Then with a hurried softness, "One kiss and the world turn crazy."

Just then it really did.

Out of the surrounding bush, a man raced to them. But then, as if he couldn't stop fast enough, the man ran right into Bill, knocking them both to the rock strewed ground.

"What the . . . what the hell is this?" Bill managed to get out as he struggled to get up.

"You bastard. She's my wife," pumped from the mouth of the other man as he tried to rise. The sweeping sound was almost overpowering, almost moving the now deadened air through audio power itself.

Jane jumped into action from a the momentary freeze of surprise. She yelled, "Fred, what the. . ." and ran to the two men, jumping on the back of the man who had rushed at them, who she now recognized as Fred, her husband. But Fred, an average sized man, abruptly stood up straight, bouncing Jane from his back, making her fall into the shallow water on the edge of the river. Bill scrambled away, frantically getting to his feet. With Jane off him, Fred immediately turned back to the man he had knocked down. He rushed at him again, this time knocking both of them into the water. And this time Bill fought. Like a squirming eel, he tried to slither away from the man who to him was a stranger, perhaps a crazy woods denizen. He stood up in the current and turned to face his attacker. As he turned he clubbed his right arm up, right into the head of the other man. The man recoiled, momentarily letting go of Bill. Then he slipped on the muddy bottom and fell into the current.

Bill stood and was about to go back fighting the man, when he thought that maybe the man needed to be helped. With that fleeting thought, he grabbed the man's leg and pulled him toward the shore. The leg responded with a kick, a kick so strong that when it hit Bill in the stomach, he went down again. Pain and a need for air took command of him. But even stronger was the need to stop the man who was now languishing in the now turbulent water.

Something strange was happening to the slough's water. Normally, placid and controlled by outtakes from the twin dams, the water now was both rising rapidly and gaining in rapidity. The usual stabilized line of shore was being engulfed by rising water, water that was in turmoil.

Bill rushed after the man, but soon he was just floating in pain and need towards the man, as they both were caught up in the current and propelled down the slough.

The man, Fred, almost in a last effort, grasped Bill extended arm and tried to pull him close. Bill fought, but he was weak from the kick he had received. He tried to use his left arm to get away from the clamp-like grip that the man had on him. But it was no use.

They both floated with increasing speed down the slough, held together by both desperation and anger.

It was then that the great swooshing occurred again and the light changed to a dreary darkness.

Chapter 55

Bobby – Thoughts of Marie

Summer School was winding down on this evening in early July, and Bobby was on the path with his skateboard. He was hoping to meet Marie, who had during the summer been walking the Sylvan Slough path after her evening meal. She walked to the Botanical Center's trail opening, not far from her home, almost always alone – although at the start she had gone with a neighborhood girlfriend, who blabbered on so much about boys that Marie just didn't call her anymore

Bobby had met her on the path a couple of times, pulling up his board and carrying it as he walked with her. Dang, she was cute, Bobby thought. And she seemed to like him – at least she went out of her way to talk to him and one time punched him in the arm in a moment of capricious jest.

"Oh, Bobby, Rock Island's Michelangelo. Whoa!"

"Hey, come on, Marie, you know I like to do stuff with the computer – stuff with drawing. You know, like that."

They bantered back and forth, just walking and talking. He had a genuine crush on her. Neat!

But this evening she didn't appear. Maybe it was the weather. Unsettled. One minute blazing summertime sun; the next a glowering of heaviness, even smelling like rain. Wait a minute. It was Tuesday. She went to band practice on Tuesday evenings. Orchestra actually.

Besides meeting Marie, he hoped somehow to meet the yellow jerseyed rider whose picture he had folded neatly in his back pocket. In his imagination he would like to question her about how she turned up looking so much like a high school girl in an old-fashioned outfit. At least he would like to see her face in real life close-up.

So it was back to skateboarding, which wasn't that bad. The slough path, as usual, was not crowded with people like the Moline path, the Butterworth. It was so bad that he had given up on it, even though it was smooth and made for nice boarding.

He took a break close to a reclaimed industrial area, now a natural park planted in wild flowers and with some of the remnants of the place's crumbled buildings still remaining. Even though the rampaging weeds were slowly easing out the wild flowers, Bobby liked it here. Occasionally he would stop and walk into the park enjoying the variegated natural plantings. He knew his friends would put him down, but he liked flowers.

But as he did so on this evening, almost abruptly the sun disappeared, overtaken by the edge of a large mass of cowering cloud, almost wispy in its substance. He turned around on a premonition and faced the slough. It was acting peculiar. He had never seen the water so high or in such rapid motion. Sure, it had rained fairly hard over the last week, but this was too much. Bobby could almost see the water rising.

It was then that he heard it – or them, or something. One was a human voice, high-pitched, caught in an extended bellow of "Fred, what the. . . " It faded followed by a confusing volume of splashing.

But what really got Bobby to become alarmed was the sound, almost eerie, of something large moving through the now gray atmosphere. Something was swooshing – up and down – hypnotizing him, rooting him to the spot.

It was then he saw the movement in the water.

Chapter 56

Bobby – to the Rescue

The swoosh resounded in Bobby's ears, the light fading as if in the heart of a cloud. Bobby sensed something was very wrong. Above the alternating sounds in the atmosphere, he heard the flailing of something big thrashing the water in front of him. Then he saw an improbable sight: two bodies rapidly floating down the slough, not together, but very close, seemingly in an attack on each other. Hands grasping and pushing, legs kicking, arms flailing.

Then the commotion stopped. No more sound; no more vociferous action. But Bobby still could see the forms moving past him. One of the bodies shifted so Bobby could see his face, and he recognized a man, a biker, who frequented the path, sometimes riding with the woman in yellow. The man seemed to be lifeless. The other form, farther away, also was inert. Bobby did not recognize the person.

But Bobby didn't hesitate. Into the water he rushed. But not for long. The slough bottom dropped off abruptly and Bobby almost submerged himself as he fought to keep his head above the surface.

He wasn't much of a swimmer, having taken some gym classes in water safety at the high school pool, but not spending much time at the city pool for recreational swimming. Bobby was more into skateboarding than swimming. But he knew how to stay above water and vaguely he remembered that the way to "save" someone was to get behind the drowning one and pull him to safety.

That's what he tried to do.

But it didn't work.

The man, the biker, put up a struggle when Bobby tried to get his right arm around the man's shoulder. In fact, he turned around in the surging water so fast that his arm in a violent surge through the water and into the air hit Bobby square in the temple.

Bobby went out – unconscious almost immediately. He would have sunk except he had managed to get a hand on the man's shirt before he was hit and his grip didn't let go. In fact it held so rigid that the man now was keeping the comatose boy from sinking. The man, Bill, didn't know this; he was trying desperately to come to his senses but was still just a floating mass hardly aware of what was going on.

The other man was nowhere to be seen.

Man and boy, Bill and Bobby, secured together by the boy's clenching hand floated down the slough as the sky became more murky and the repetitive zooming sounds of great motion filled the narrow line of fast moving water.

Bill could not keep himself afloat. He slowly sank lower into the water.

Bobby's hand with it claw-like grip relaxed and he too sank. The two forms separated.

Chapter 57

Roger – to the Rescue

Roger's transformation continued. From being almost a non-person in his life-long odyssey around the country, he now was becoming a person of worth, even action. From being the target of a couple of thieves out for a few bucks from a bum on the path, he was now going to "get 'em." He set out to patrol the Sylvan Slough path, being much more careful and observant than his usual almost thoughtless meandering. And tied on the back of his bike was a sturdy piece of driftwood, smooth and hard as a rock, about 3 feet long. He was not going to be unarmed.

On this particularly fine summer evening, he started out from his apartment with sunshine as bright in his face as a floodlight on a stage. But as he traveled down the path from Schwiebert Park, a sudden upsurge of dark clouds dimmed the light behind him. And in front a mist was rising, slight, but with a movement to it. It seemed to Roger to be moving in a undulating fashion, swelling and contracting, but getting incrementally darker as he traveled into it.

He was preoccupied with the sides of the path, not wanting to be surprised as he was before by the two ruffians who from what they said before Roger curled into a ball of negativity had been following him, had thought that he had more to steal than the few dollars they wrested from his pocket.

Nearing the site of his old cave, he decided to see if he could catch them by going down to the banks of the slough and then watching the path from below. He hid his bike in the shrubbery, took his bat, and maneuvered down the steep gradient to the water. New plant growth and a higher level of water in the slough almost prevented him from recognizing the place, but at the bottom he recognized the slight opening that led to the old cave.

He ignored it, not wanting to be near it if something happened.

But as he was moving through the scrabbled rocks, weeds, and spindly scrubs above the shoreline, he heard a high pitched female voice yelling, something like "Ned . . . What ...?" He saw some sort of commotion across the slough at the point where the two streams surrounding the island came together.

But he hardly had time to consider the yell or the activity. Instead he was instantly engulfed with a nightmare, his own particular nightmare. A boy was floating past him, a boy who appeared to be Troy Yelkin, his schoolboy companion from so many years ago.

Roger was struck dumb and immobile. He stared and his brain emptied of everything except the memories of that horrible day in just about the same place as now. The boy, if it were truly a boy, floated swiftly, but without motion past him. Roger was cataleptic. Was this some dim judgment being thrust upon him? Was he being, some how, brought back to how his life was ruined, and his friend from the past was killed.

Then he remembered. "I killed him. I pushed him and made him fall and hit his head." The enormity of it swooped over him like a cloud of pewter colored mist.

But he stopped. He woke from the spell. A cry broke the grip of the memories - because another body was floating down the slough, this one large and splashing, and struggling to be vocal.

This time Roger didn't hesitate. He ran through the water until he had to swim, and swim he did to the struggling man. He grasped him underneath the man's armpits, and tugged him to shore.

Thus Roger met Bill.

And when Roger was sure that Bill, although hardly moving, was alive and conscious, he scrambled up the slight bluff, got on his creaky old bike, and started after the major image in his mind – a young boy floating – floating   down   the   rampaging   slough.

Chapter 58

Duane – "stalking" Jane

Duane kept the faded water bottle in the bottom drawer of the chest in his bedroom, the place for sweaters that he had worn for many years but now were close to being worn out. But he liked them and refused to throw them away. He always said that he would wear them when he did odd jobs, but he never did.

But now the bottle was in the back of the drawer, a secret place, almost a revered place containing a holy icon.

Nonsense, he told himself. You're a mature man with a responsible job. You shouldn't be acting like a gawky teenager going crazy over the new girl in class.

But he was.

For one thing, he had controlled himself to use his binoculars on her bike rather than her as she sped by on the path. After two attempts he was almost one-hundred per-cent sure that the bottle was hers, because an identical one, except for being brightly colored, was held securely in the bottle rack on her bike.

And for another thing, he was becoming a stalker – somewhat. He knew that if she did her usual ride, she would be riding downriver in the evening as the sun was setting. She either left the trail somewhere down there and rode home, or she had a car parked somewhere. He wanted to find it – or if she rode home, to trail her home.

So Duane, when he saw her pedaling on the path going upstream, left the office as early as he could and drove down to the most logical place for her to leave the path – Schwiebert Park. He parked in the small lot and took a seat on a park bench with a view of the path, which skirted the edge of the park right next to the railroad tracks.

He missed her on the first two times he did it. But on the third, a brilliant crystal clear evening with a vibrant sunset hovering like a sunflower on the horizon, she passed him. She did not stop or swerve away from the path to ride through the downtown of Rock Island – to go home or to get to her car.

She continued down the trail, past the park and the imposing Modern

Woodman Insurance building which commandeered a long portion of the riverfront, just to the east of the Centennial Bridge between Rock Island and Davenport.

Duane knew that there were very few places to leave the path until close to its end. And the only places with parking lots were at Sunset Park – either the fishing access at one end of the park or the end of the trail at the other. Accordingly he parked at the fishing access, down a short slope from the trail, and kept a secret eye out for anyone using the trail above. The first time he did this, he was successful. She, to him a beautiful yellow streak of hallowed harmony, sped right by him.

Two evenings later he was in the small parking lot at the very end of the path. He knew she was on the path and he was waiting. Not wanting to be conspicuous in his car, he draped his binoculars on his shoulder and walked along the roadway and an adjacent road leading to a marina, pretending to be a bird watcher.

And it was true. He was watching for his yellow bird.

And he found her.

He was close enough that he could see the entire area of the parking lot without his binoculars. By being discrete, he was sure he would be able to see if she had a car or continued biking on an access road leading to the city.

But to his chagrin another biker was with her – the same man who he had noticed a number of times riding with her – and one time right in front of his office they had stopped and had a fairly long talk. Now this man rode right behind her as she approached a light blue, fairly new Honda Insight with a bike rack on its back. She made preparations for mounting the bike while chatting with the man, who was undistinguished except for a slight familiarity in his face. Duane felt that he had seen him some place before – not on a bike and not on the path.

But Duane didn't stop and gawk. He didn't want to be noticed. However, now he knew her vehicle.

The next day he nonchalantly strolled through the parking lot before she arrived and noted the license plate on the blue Honda.

That same night he was on his home computer and by checking a few official Illinois sites knew her name and address. She was Jane Tressel and she married to Fred Tressel. With Google he quickly found out that she worked at a Rock Island ad agency and was an executive administrator .

Duane was somewhat deflated. The mystery was taken out of his dream girl. She was real – she had a name and an identity.

But then something happened that changed his life completely.

It happened at work – close to the end of his shift - on the path right in front of him and it not only brought back all the old complexity of that floating body years ago, but peering through his binoculars, Duane saw a floating body.

And it was the floating body of a boy.

Chapter 59

Duane leaps in

This time he didn't hesitate. Duane rushed from his office and, except for flinging off his shoes, leapt into the water that was now higher than he had ever seen it. And it was moving quickly downstream with a fierceness that belied its usual calm nature.

He didn't care that what had been a sunny nightfall had turned suddenly into drab, overcast murk. He was not concerned about the clothes he was wearing – hardly giving them even a thought.

What caught him up was the churning water ahead of him. Where had the body gone? He knew he has seen it floating at a fairly fast pace just to the right of his office viewing window. And he knew that it hadn't taken him very long to get to the shore of the slough. It should be in front of him. He was sure.

Now dog paddling in the increasingly deepening water the whole memory of the first time this had happened came back to him. And as his eyes searched frantically, it was his indecision that returned with a powerful thrust. He hadn't responded the first time he has seen a body floating by from his window. He had been mesmerized by fear. Now, so much older, he had learned. He was in the water actively trying to help.

Duane was a decent swimmer – or at least he had been in his youth and young adulthood when he spent much time at the municipal swimming pool on a major hill in Rock Island.

Now he saw the water give way.

Something emerged from the rippling surface, slowly revealing a form.

Duane stopped paddling and stared. Was this now or then. He was seeing the floating body of a youngster, a body floating face down, with the back of its neck as white as a brand new tee shirt.

But, no, this was now. No indecision now. He was in the water, wet, and within swimming distance of the body.

He stopped dog paddling and with arms cramped somewhat by his long sleeved shirt, swam out to the body.

Almost exhausted, but he was successful in pulling the limp young boy from the surging water.

He dragged him up to the muddy shore, now more bushes than stone and gravel, and attempted to do CPR on the comatose body. But Duane really didn't know what he was doing – it had been years since he had read about the procedure and gone to a demonstration of it during a work education session.

But now as he was bringing up the boy's arms from behind, the boy opened his mouth and a flood of water erupted from it. The boy, who was Bobby Scott, coughed and retched and Duane could see his right eye flutter. Then the boy pushed on the ground with his hands and raised himself up, turning over so that he was sitting.

He coughed then said, "Where's the man?"

Duane said, "What do you mean, 'Where's the man?'"

"There was a man. I was with him, trying to get him to breathe in the water. Where is he?"

"I pulled you out . . . but I didn't see anyone else. There was no one else with you."

"He kicked me, but I held on to him."

"No. No one was with you."

"Then it got dim . . . and I don't know what happened. Maybe I let go. I don't know. But I know that I was floating with the man – a biker. He bikes around here a lot."

Just then they were interrupted by a plaintive cry coming from up-river. It was Jane, but they did not recognize her voice, so strained and harsh was it. "Bill, Bill. And Fred, Where are you. Come back. Please." The "Please" was dragged out into an extended anguished cry.

Duane said to the sitting boy. "You stay here, right here. Don't move. I'll be right back. You heard that. That woman's in need."

He turned from the boy and walked back into the water, walking along its side, going up river towards the bridge to Sylvan Island. He kept watch at the other side of the slough, at the island's shore until he saw her, a woman at the point of the island. And it was his Yellow Bird, standing crestfallen and in distress.

He turned and went into the deluge, focusing on a point to the east of her because he was being carried forcefully by the current. He was tired; he was not used to such vigorous effort, was not in shape for it. But he did make it to the other side, a distance of not even a tenth of a mile.

Chapter 60

Jane - Dumbfounded

Soaked and amazed, Jane was dumbfounded. Surrounded by a sudden thrust of nature's chaos – darkening gloom, blowing sound, and rampaging water – she was at a loss. She just stood, ankle deep in the rising water which before was two feet from her.

She was alone. Bill and her husband, Fred, both gone, somewhere in the slough. She said to herself that she should go to their aid. But a stubborn fact countered that. She could not swim. She had never learned, and in fact was terrified by free water. In high school she got an exception to the swimming session of the gym class, going completely to pieces when she was ordered into the pool. After an agonizing session with the whistle obsessed gym teacher, she was transferred to a different gym class for the time when she should have been in the pool.

So now Jane just stood in rising terror.

Suddenly a man loomed in front of her, rising out of the water like a sunken buoy suddenly released. The man, wearing ordinary office clothes, wiped his face, saw her on the shore, and yelled: "Are you OK? I heard your yell."

"I'm OK, yes. But two men are in the river – caught up in it. They're gone. I can't see them."

"Two men? No, no, no. A boy. It was a boy. I pulled him out. He's OK . . . on the shore."

"No it's two men. One is my husband."

"I heard you yell . . . before. So I came . . . through the water. It was tough. I've never seen a current like this."

The man, who was Duane, sloshed through the mucky slough bottom towards Jane, but just as his chest was level with the water's surface, he slipped on something on the river bottom and the force of the water pushed him into the current again.

Duane, who had pulled Bobby to safety, was now himself rolling down the current, submerged, and unable to right himself. He tried to swim and get his head above water, but he had been weakened by the evenings events.

He was swept away.

Chapter 61

Jane - to the Rescue

Then abruptly Jane bawled out to the world: "What the hell am I doing!" With that she jumped up, ran to her bike, and took off up the dirt path to the bridge. The men in her life – and another who she didn't even know - needed help and she couldn't swim. She would look for them as she biked along the slough. Maybe she could find them and bring them to shore – or help them if they had made it to shore.

The light was still deepening and her vision was labored, but she could keep an eye on the water as she biked along. Just about at the point of the path were the old industry park joined it, she noticed someone on a bike ahead of her. It was a man, but not a biker in jersey and bike shorts. All she saw was a blur of vague brown, but the man was traveling fast and in a funny way. She recognized something about him that took her back in time. And way in the distance a figure, possibly a female, was vigorously walking in her direction.

Just then Bill stumbled onto the path.

He was completely wet, hair plastered to his head, and he was frantic.

"Jane. Thank god. We have to get some help here. A man's in the water, the guy who was fighting with me. Wait a minute. There's a kid too. A kid was next to me in the water, I'm sure."

She dropped her bike on the side and frantically searched the pocket in back of her jersey for her cell phone. She found it and started punching 911 only to get nothing. It had been submerged when she was in the water.

"It's not working. Oh, damn, I can't get anything out of it."

Bill almost yelled at her. "We've got to get downriver. That water's going so fast, those guys won't make it. They'll be swept away."

"Are you all right, Bill?"

"I guess so, even though I can hardly walk."

Jane grabbed his arm and said, "I'll go – on my bike – I'll find them."

They heard a scrambling in the underbrush. Two hands appeared, then two arms. It was Bobby.

He softly said, "The guy said for me to stay there, right where I was. The guy who pulled me out of the river. But I heard you and I left."

Bill exploded, "You're the kid, the kid who was hanging on to me."

"Yeah, and you're the biker. I was trying to help . . . trying to pull you out."

The figure who had been walking towards them, now started to run.

Bobby let out a yell, "Marie, you're here. You're not wet are you? You're OK, right?"

Marie almost yelled: "We got out of band early so here I am. What's going on?"

Bill interrupted, "Hey, do you have a cell phone?"

Marie nodded, "Yeah, sure. You want to make a call?"

"Call 911. There's a guy in the water, caught in the current. Here, give me the phone. I'll try to explain."

Jane interrupted, "Bill, there's more than one man in the water. Back there, a man tried to help me and he was swept away . . . swept away right at the tip of that island."

Bobby now interrupted, "Was he a . . . a middle aged man, looking like an office worker. Yeah, did he have an ID tag on?"

Jane said, "I was too far away to tell, but, yeah, he did look like an office worker, although he was all wet – oh, and I would say he was middle aged. But Fred – my husband – is still in the river. I've got to go to him, to find him. You stay here and wait for the responders. I'm taking off."

With that, she was on her bike, pedaling rapidly down the trail, keeping an eye on the waters of the surging slough as well as she could. She knew there were possibly two men in the water – one of them someone who emerged from the river unexpectedly and then was gone in a swift watery second. The other man was her husband, Fred.

Chapter 62

Roger – He Bikes to the Rescue

Roger, now was frantically pedaling his rusty old Schwinn 10-speed down the path. He had left Bill, gasping for air and looking completely exhausted, on the shore because he was sure he had seen another person in the water, floating amid the churning stream. And the person was a boy. Or was he just hallucinating? Was he just bringing up that event that had stood so tall in his life – the death of his schoolboy friend, Troy. Or, as he constantly thought, the murder of Troy by himself when the two of them were having a kid's fit way back then.

But, nevertheless, now he rode fast – possibly faster than he had ever biked in his life. He had to find that boy. Nature, however, seemed to be doing everything to prevent him from finding the boy. Twilight, almost darkness; wild swooshing sounds and noise; and a roiling mass of water spilling down the slough. It was hard for him to both bike hard and also keep an eye on the water's surface, searching for any trace of the boy.

He hit the end of the slough where its waters joined with the major Mississippi river coming through the dam joining Arsenal Island with Davenport. He considered for a moment just stopping and waiting to see if the boy would be floating by. But the water was moving so fast that he was afraid that he was too late – that the boy was past him.

Roger made a quick decision. He went on, pedaling quickly and searching the wide expanse of water, which was calmer now, the slough's sudden impetus of water slowed as it joined the much greater Mississippi.

Roger sped to the little park at 20th Street, where he stopped and surveyed the wide water. It was moving, but he couldn't see anything that even resembled a form in the water, not even a floating log. At Schwiebert Park he did just about the same thing: stopped, looked closely, and found nothing. He was perturbed that he could not see clearly across the expanse, the light was fading so fast.

But he was frantic. What if he had missed him? What if he were way down the river, floating and drowning at this moment?

Back on the bike, he maneuvered through the park. He swept past the large insurance building and parking lot which prevented him for seeing the river, and went up a slight rise to levee height right after going under the Centennial Bridge. Here he could again see the complete river.

But, as he stopped at a small rest area with one park bench, there was nothing – at least as far as he could readily see. If the boy had somehow moved across the water on to the Iowa side, all Roger's speeding would be for naught.

He kept on, however. The levee path now was straight and clear, and he could eyeball the river often through gaps in the tree-line.

All at once, just before he reached the railroad bridge, the darkness eased up somewhat. The heavy clouds skittered away from the setting sun, only a few tendrils masking the dying rays. Roger dipped down to another resting place almost under the bridge, and there he was.

He found a body, a listless form on the rock-strewn shoreline.

Jumping off his bike, he rushed to the body, turned it over, and realized that it wasn't a boy. It was a full grown adult, an older man – a man dressed like an office worker, a man with a pin on his upper chest that read: Duane Holstrom.

Chapter 63

Jane – Finds the rescued Duane

A Moline police car along with an ATV equipped with rescue gear found the three people - Bill, Bobby, and Marie – as they were walking up the path, going to the Sylvan Island bridge after Bill had made the 911 call. Both Bill and Bobby were very slow, the effects of being in the torrent of water. Surviving half under the surface had drained their physical resources.

Bobby, however, was a little more alert than Bill because Marie was holding his hand. It happened unexpectedly, just after Jane had taken off on her bike looking for the men in the water. Bobby had sat down in the middle of the path, looking grimly to the west, into what should have been the setting sun. Bill didn't sit, but he was just about as lethargic as Bobby.

Marie rose to the occasion. She grabbed Bobby hand and pulled. It was the impetus he needed. He rose.

She said, "Come on. We should go down to the park down there."

She led the way, and they were just about to the park and its bridge to Sylvan Island when the authorities found them.

The patrol officer in the police car first called for an ambulance when he saw the debilitated condition of the two males and heard a brief summary of what they had been through.

Marie spoke up: "There was a lady here who said two more people are in the river. She took off on her bike to try to find them. They need help."

The officer immediately radioed the Rock Island Police and sent the ATV down the path to give any help it could.

In the meantime, Jane was pedaling and looking - to no avail. Two men. Her husband who rushed at Bill in a fit of anger and sent them both to the water. And the mysterious man who had surfaced from the water in front of her. But she could see no trace of either of them.

As she was going under the Centennial Bridge in Rock Island, she noticed flashing lights behind her and soon realized that a police car was on the path behind her. As she looked ahead, she saw a number of people next to the river in a small rest area. They were looking down; one of them kneeling, she felt her heart bind up. "They found him. They found Fred."

She biked down the slight slope to the rest area, almost flew off her bike, and came up to the gathering. The three men parted and she looked down at the man who was still gasping for air.

He was a middle aged man wearing office clothes, the same man who earlier had unexpectedly risen from the water at Sylvan Island.

It wasn't Fred.

No bike was in sight; the three men, she found out later, were not path users. They were watchmen on the railroad bridge overhead who had seen what had happened and rushed to help.

Soon both an ambulance and a police car arrived, along with an ATV with two rescue people. They made sure the man was OK, and then carried him to the ambulance for a ride to a hospital.

Jane adamantly told the emergency people that her husband was not accounted for – either still in the river or somewhere clinging to the shore.

Soon a full-scale operation was in progress, complete with observers on both sides of the river, a number of volunteer boats, and even a Coast Guard boat complete with a powerful searchlight. Most of the boats headed up river; downriver because of the darkness was not promising. The river was wide and light was fleeting.

A decision was made to explore the Slough fully, but hold off on the major river until the morning.

While all of this was going on, Jane asked the railroad workers if they had seen anyone pull the man out of the river.

One of them said, "Yeah, some homeless guy found him. The guy was on an old rusty bike, but he was going real fast down the trail. He lucked out and found this guy floating in the river."

Jane asked, "And where is this guy? Where is he now?"

"He ain't here, ma'am. He took off almost as soon as he had the guy on land. He looked pretty scruffy, but, hey, he might have saved that guy's life. That's something. Yeah, that's something to be proud of."

Chapter 64

Fred's Finish

Fred Tressel was never seen again in the Quad Cities.

He disappeared despite an extensive search operation that involved alerting river agencies all the way from Rock Island to the confluence of the Mississippi and Ohio rivers. Dredging took place in some areas, but authorities soon realized that it was too hit-or-miss. The river is full of islands, sloughs, off-shoots, bends, sandbars, and much debris. Unspoken was the almost sure knowledge that a dead body, drowned in the river, would surface at some time and at some place – where, it would be impossible to tell.

Then in the middle of October, almost three and a half months after the incident in Sylvan Slough, two men fishing from a powerboat near Keokuk, Iowa – and full of beer on a sunny afternoon – accidentally ran their boat into a woody embankment and penetrated through a built-up cover of dead tree limbs into a break in the shoreline, a concave depression in the bank-side dirt that was also just slightly above the surface of the water.

As they tried to reverse their boat and get back into the main river, the man who had drunk only four of the cans from the twelve pack, yelled, "Whoa. Hold off. There's something in there. Let's take a look."

He got out and waded into the opening. He found what appeared to be a pile of men's clothing and a powerful smell.

He had found Fred Tressel. - or, more accurately, the remains of Fred Tressel.

Chapter 65

Jane

In the months after the Sylvan Slough "incident" Jane was distraught – but at the same time very energetic in trying to find out anything about her missing husband. In fact, she was obsessed: she led, pushed, goaded, or did everything she could think of to come up with anything related to the disappearance. She convinced many private boat people up and down the river – along with all of the official safety and emergency agencies – to go out of their way to search for traces or anything out of the ordinary. She spent her weekends on the river, finding cooperative boat owners to ferry her around. But, alas, she found nothing.

She resisted the urge – so prevalent before the incident – to seek companionship with Bill. Their romance – if it were really a romance – ended. They couldn't help seeing each other – both professionally, as her ad agency was developing a campaign for his bank, and recreationally as they did their biking in the morning and evening – but they didn't go on group rides together or even meet each other on a casual basis. Their kissing episodes evaporated.

She became a sort of guardian angel to Bobby Scott, who along with Bill and Duane Holstrom, were recovered from their near drownings during the incident.

She became especially close to Bobby after he showed her his picture of her as a young Emily in "Our Town" so many years ago. - the picture he had altered to age her and to show the basic resemblance that she still had to her teen-age self. She came to his house to see how he was doing and was struck when she met his mother. She recognized her. "Wait a minute, I think I remember you. You're, ah, let me think. Marcie, Marcie Scott. But, may I ask, what was your name before you were married?

"Oh, I grew up as Marcie Yelkin. That was my maiden name before I married my first husband. Now I'm Marcie Scott – been so for 15 years now."

"Oh, my god. Marcie Yelkin. I remember now. You were the sister of that boy who disappeared from . . ." Here she stopped and just stared at the mother and then the son. "The boy, the 11-year-old boy who drowned in the slough, or at least was never found."

Bobby's mother just looked at her.

Jane continued, "I remember. His name was Troy, Troy Yelkin I was ahead of him in school a year or two. Oh," Here she rushed to Marcie and embraced her. "Oh, I'm sorry to even bring this up. I'm sure you feel real bad about it."

Marcie Scott in the midst of the embrace, stared straight ahead and all at once burst out, "That slough! That god-damn slough. My brother and now – almost – my boy."

She pushed Jane away from her and went to Bobby, grabbing him by the shoulders with her two hands and pushed her face close to his. "Promise me, Bobby. Promise me you'll never go down to that slough again. That you've got to promise me." She held him and kept eye contact until he responded.

"OK, mom. I understand. I get it. No more Sylvan Slough for me. I get it now. Just about the same thing happened to your brother as almost happened to me – drowning in the slough."

His mother just stared at him and softly said, "Promise. Promise, please."

Bobby was almost crying. "I do, Mom. I will. No more. No more slough for me."

And Bobby was true to his promise. He never again walked, skateboarded, or biked the Sylvan Slough trail.

Jane also visited Duane Holstrom in the hospital when he was recovering, leading to an instant friendship between the two of them – a friendship based on reality, not on the dream-like adoration that had captured Duane before. Every time she saw him, and she would pop into his office occasionally after he was back at work, the first thing that came into her head was the memory of the "homeless" man who had been riding his old bike so fast on the evening of the incident. Something about the fleeting glimpse brought a wealth of feeling back to her – feelings from the past. That homeless man had saved Duane and then, almost as fast as he appeared at just the right moment, he had disappeared. No one could identify him definitely, and he never showed up in any of the investigations that took place after the incident.

And, as it turned out, neither Jane or anyone else knew that the "homeless" man had saved Bill's life, had pulled him out of the stream of water, had made sure he was alive and breathing on the shore of the slough, and then had rushed to his bike to see if he could find the young boy who he had seen being propelled downstream by the raging current.

Jane never knew that the "homeless" man was the brother she had not heard from for the greater part of her life, the brother who she assumed was lost forever to her. She occasionally thought of him – especially after her father's funeral, which came almost two years after the death of her mother.

She was left alone, but in six months after her dad's funeral she had married Fred in a minimal ceremony at the county office building. Throughout her marriage, her brother was relegated back and back farther into the dimness of her past. She had basically given up ever seeing him again or finding out what had happened to him – until, that is, the fleeting glimpse of the man racing ahead of her on the slough.

Chapter 66

The Mysterious Incident

The incident caused certain controversy in the area around Sylvan Slough. No one could fully explain it. The light, certainly, was no problem. Clouds, including rain clouds, come and go. The intensity of the light was commonly attributed to the contrast between the full setting sun and the suddenly dark clouds cutting it off. But the speed at which the cutting occurred caused meteorologists to hedge their conclusions.

No one, however, could make sense of the sounds that those on the slough that evening heard. To most of those interviewed it was unearthly – a wavering, slicing sound. It was as if something was enveloping them, or at least their head and ears. They felt they were being invisibly pounded by sheer movement. Interviewers asked people who were on other parts of the Great River Trail that evening if they had heard anything. The invariable answer was, "What sound? I didn't hear anything." People who lived in the area reported nothing also. One bike rider who just happened to be on the Sylvan Slough portion of the the trail, did say he had heard a different sound, but thought it was some machinery in a factory or something accidentally happening at one of the shipping companies in the area.

The torrent of water, however, was inexplicable. It was there; it was real. But how and why? Government officials on Arsenal Island consulted with the lock and dam bridge tenders. They reported a slight rise in the water level – due to the minor summer flooding from the rain of the previous week. The power dam tenders on the other side of the island – and the ones in charge of the power company's dam between Moline and the island also reported just a slight rise. Instruments at all three of the dams confirmed what the tenders said: just a slight rise

But it wasn't a slight rise. It was a major cascade of water, rampaging down the slough. This was determined when investigators examined the banks of the slough and found major erosion and flattening out of stream side vegetation. And they determined that it was almost completely confined to the actual slough. The riversides of the main river to the west of Arsenal Island showed no signs of high water levels – not even a water line higher than it had been.

The onrush of water had happened. Arsenal officials could not deny that. In fact Jerry O'Malley, who had the watch the evening of the incident at the power dam, was put on indefinite leave on the day after it happened. He told his superiors that he had not noticed anything unusual except for the sudden darkening of the setting sun. Had he heard the strange sound? He could not remember it. (He did not tell anyone that he had been watching an episode of The Jerry Springer Show when it happened.) Nevertheless, he never returned to that post – taking early retirement at the request of the officials.

The incident remained a mystery. And it remained that way even after the body of Fred Tressel was found way down near Keokuck, Iowa.

Oh, one other thing: Mountain bikers on Sylvan Island reported that one of their single-track trails on the west side of the island was blocked by a large number of fallen tree limbs. No trees were down or uprooted, but many showed considerable damage from limbs snapped off or torn away. Was it caused by a sudden gust of wind? There was no evidence of that.

What happened that evening on Sylvan Slough remained mysterious. And it is so to this day.

Epilog - Duane

In the aftermath of the events on Sylvan Slough Duane Holstrom became a local hero. Bobby Scott told the police and the rescue responders that he had been saved by a middle aged man dressed in office clothing, who as soon as Bobby was safe on shore, ran to the aid of a woman's voice cutting through the swooshing sound around them. He did not know who the man was, but in a later match-up at the hospital, identified Duane as the man who pulled him to safety.

Jane also identified Duane as the man who seemingly mysteriously rose from the water to come to her aid, only to be swept away by the suddenly raging torrent.

A reporter from the Rock Island Argus interviewed Duane after he had returned home, but before he went back to work. Yes, Duane indeed jumped into the water to try to save the young boy, who turned out to be Bobby Scott. Then, when he heard cries from a female, he also went to her aid. But as he was approaching her through the slough waters, he slipped and the current dragged him into the middle of the stream with so much force that he could hardly move his limbs, much less swim.

The newspaper reporter, than checked with both Bobby and Jane and wrote up a long account that made the front page of the paper on the day after the Fourth of July.

Duane's life was turned around. Instead of being a nondescript freight dispatcher, he was now a community hero. At the end of that summer he was summoned to Rock Island's city hall where he, along with three other citizen (including Bobby Scott), was given a certificate in recognition of their coming to the aid of their fellow man.

When the words on Duane's certificate were read, he choked up. He could hardly thank the mayor and city council for the honor. Then, after staring at the opposite wall of the city council chambers, he blurted out the following:

"You say I'm a hero. Well . . . I'm no hero. I let him go by. I didn't help. I didn't go after him. That boy, many years ago, that boy, Troy Yelkin. the one who disappeared. He went right by me, and I didn't help. I just watched and was frozen." Here he paused and tears started to flow. "I didn't move. And the kid just went right by. So I'm no hero. Here, take this certificate. It says I'm a hero, but I'm not." He broke down and the mayor had to escort him from the front of the room.

But that wasn't the end of it. The next day, the same Argus reporter wrote up the entire story and it again made the front page. This time the story of the "Hesitant Hero" was picked up by the wire services and Duane became somewhat of a national celebrity. He even was invited to Chicago for a couple of interviews on regional television. He didn't go, but one of them, WGN, came to Rock Island and interviewed him.

He was awkwardly reluctant to talk about what he had done – and he always also applauded what Bobby Scott had attempted to do.

In the days that followed, Duane still remained at his old job, but now he had gained the esteem of his fellow employees, especially Wilbur.

He never married. But the one genuine satisfaction he received from the whole incident was the occasional visit to him made by Jane. He didn't adore her anymore, but she became a confidante and, from what she told him, a close friend. And, as it turned out, after it was formed, he became vice president of the "Sylvan Slough White Swan Project," a community improvement group headed by Jane.

Epilog – Bobby

Bobby and Marie became boy friend - girl friend for almost a year after they had walked hand in hand down the Sylvan Slough path to meet the emergency team.

But it didn't last.

Marie, as it turned out - with her braces removed and hair, clothes, and makeup styling aided by Bobby's skilled graphic representations - matured into a stunning beauty. Before her junior year at Rock Island High School, she tried out for the varsity cheer-leading squad and made it with ease and aplomb. She also blossomed into quite an outgoing personality, almost a complete turnaround from what she was as a freshman. And she excelled in academics. In short, she became the epitome of the well-rounded high school student – and graduate. She went to the University of Illinois at Champaign majoring in chemical engineering. After graduation, she worked in Chicago for Eli Lily, helping produce a major breakthrough in the sanitation of landfills. Alas, just as she had finally met the man of her dreams, her Ford Fiesta was obliterated and she was killed instantaneously in an accident on the Dan Ryan Expressway. Bobby, who had occasionally stopped in at her parents' home in Rock Island, was hit hard by her death, the first to happen to those he knew from high school.

Bobby became a secondary local media hero after that tragic evening on the slough. At first investigators wondered what he was doing in the slough's waters. Then when it became apparent, from Bill's and his own account of the event, that he had risked his life to go to the aid of two men floating down the stream, he was linked with Duane as one of the two slough heroes. He, reluctantly, was also present at the city council citizen hero presentation and he accepted his certificate with just a few quiet words of thanks.

At his high school graduation, he was honored by being named the best senior artist. The award came with a five-hundred dollar scholarship, which after much deliberation he used for his first semester to the Belvedere Art Academy in Des Moines, Iowa. He attended the college for two years before moving back to Rock Island to work as a graphic designer for Haver, Osborne, and Teakon, Jane's ad agency. He married the girl he had started dating a few months after Marie drifted away from him, and they settled into a comfortable life in Rock Island.

He, along with Jane, became very friendly with Duane, the man who he always claimed saved his life.. And every Thanksgiving and Christmas Duane was an honored guest at their house, which eventually also included four children. Uncle Duane became almost the kids' real uncle.

Jane was also a major part of his life. He worked and thrived at her ad agency, and with the creation of the Sylvan Slough White Swan Project he created all of the graphics – award winning, as it turned out – for the area-wide innovative community action group.

Epilog – Bill

Bill never knew for sure who had saved his life. He had a dim memory of fighting while the water swirled around him, trying to keep afloat while someone was pulling on him, someone smaller than he. The last he remembered before he went under and lost consciousness was a bigger person pulling him. But that was that. He could remember nothing else until he recovered on the shore of Sylvan Slough.

He spent two days at the Trinity Hospital after the incident. He had been severely tested physically, but mentally he was much more in jeopardy. For one thing, he couldn't get his first live-in girl friend, Lila Shory, and what had happened to her, out of his mind. His long held back feeling of guilt about her tragic death now surfaced and rammed head-on into what happened with Jane on the eventful evening on the slough.

He mind spiraled with guilt.

Had somehow his kissing of her had anything to do with the resulting catastrophe?

After leaving the hospital, he spent two days at his house recuperating, but also coming to terms with the experience. Even though he was committed to Jane, possibly even in love with her, he resolved at the end of the second day, to give her up. Helping considerably with the decision was the fact that Fred Tressel was still missing. Also he had heard that Jane was frantic in trying to find her husband. Bill knew that he just couldn't complicate things by reaching to her again.

Recovered and back at work and settled into his relatively new job as bank Vice President, becoming with his innovations in marketing and his dedication to hard work, an up-and-coming leader in the local banking community. He continued to work with Jane's ad agency, but the contact between the two of them was minimal. The agency's staff took over the day-to-day tasks of putting it all together for the bank.

As the years went on, he became the epitome of the respected and competent bank executive. But he was not happy. He dated occasionally, especially when community dinners and such events demanded his presence, but even the energetic owner of an up-start digital software company, Beth Plover, couldn't gain his utmost attention.

And he became a regular member of the "Ash Wednesday Club," an informal gathering of professional people that started after working hours at a local pub, the Oasis, on a Wednesday in April that just happened to be Ash Wednesday. The "club" grew until it became the place to meet the rising set who made things work in the downtown area. Jane, obviously, became a regular – but only occasionally gave attention to Bill. And he held himself back similarly.

After the incident, unfortunately, his life was a matter of running in place, or, if you will, of spinning on his bicycle, not the full fun of taking his gears to their fulfillment. Always in the back of his mind were the two women who he had somehow jeopardized with tragic results.

He became a successful, but unrealized – and unhappy – man.

But that, as it turned out, was not to be.

Epilog – Jane

Jane, on the other hand, rebounded with vigor after the recovery of the body of her dead husband and his funeral. She was not filled with sorrow as Bill was. For one thing, after Fred's office returned all of Fred's personal effects to her, she became even more beyond sorrow.

Fred had left her, accidentally, a digital legacy of betrayal.

His personal laptop, only minimally protected by passwords, showed, after she had also found his series of weak passwords in the notebooks also returned to her, that he had been unfaithful to her in the months preceding his death. In fact, as she delved more and more into his past, she found that during almost his whole life with her, he had been having affairs, flings, and other assorted extra-marital adventures.

In fact, when she visited his office to sign some legal papers in relation to his company insurance, she felt a strange aura as she entered the office space. Three of the workers stared at her almost open-mouthed. One of them, an obviously fake breasted, and heavily made-up past-thirty woman with a seemingly perpetual sneer, seemed to be putting a hex on her. Jane left as soon as possible, but not without enduring the uninterrupted stares of all of the three.

How could she have been so ignorant. As she looked back, much of her past life with Fred fell into place. His late nights at work. His company mandated trips to Las Vegas, New York City, and other places. His becoming irritated at many minor happenings in their common life. But mainly his estrangement to her and her more energetic ways.

She came into her own even more than before. Besides her work, which was growing to the point where she had to hire a personal dedicated assistant, she started to take on many community and volunteer responsibilities. For instance, the local "Play It Again," an amateur theatrical group, became almost financially viable because of her heading its fund raising efforts. She even co-starred in one of its plays, portraying a slutty tramp in a Western drama about lost dreams.

She also re-met, as she called it in her imagination, Bill. They slowly drifted back together – the Ash Wednesday fun helped much – until they became a steady couple for three years. Then, with just a small ceremony, they were married.

Epilog - Roger

Fat black birds – craven crows, cruelly obese, jawed and cawed on the fine narrow path. Sauntering through the grass next to the slough, they spat at him with black flings of contempt. He ignored their caterwauling. They cawed; he wauled.

He had important things to do. But oddly, their constant cacophony was in syncopation with him. Their stridency echoed his.

He pushed harder on his pedals, increased his speed, traveled.

They bawled after him – even after he had gone under the bridge to the Rock Island Arsenal and up the levee embankment. With a quick jerk of a look, he caught just a glimpse of their fluttery abruptness. His affinity vanished. They seemed to be pursuing.

Roger Pice rode on.

A woman bicyclist in a yellow jersey, no markings on it, loomed ahead, converging on him, riding right down the faded center line of the levee path. Drop-offs on both sides prevented any radical swerves, so he yelled: "Hey, I'm here." Why he said that, he did not know. But it was apropos. "I am here." For now.

Out popped a quick "Woops" from her as she braked, stopping completely just as he passed her. A hint of recognition from both of them surfaced. He was temped to also stop and question her, but he let it go.

Just then he heard another sound – a very faint reverberating drumming, more of a staccato ping than a boom or a rat-a-tat. Was it a frog? Was it the clucking of some kind of a bird? Was it some living thing lurking around this backwater of faded industry. Or was it something within him?

Recently he'd been bothered. Sometimes he found himself wide awake looking at the his faded, undistinguished room and hearing something strange in the hollow of his body, something that he could not place.

But now he said to himself: "Aw, wait a minute. It's fireworks. Kids setting off strings of firecrackers. It's the Fourth of July. Just the way-off noise of some poppers."

And yet!

Underneath the railroad bridge he almost hit a fisherman coming down the path. Why hadn't he seen the paunchy, beer-bellied man carrying a plastic five-gallon can and a couple of rods and reels? What made the man almost leap into the path right in front of him? Didn't he see him coming?

Up and back on the levee, he heard the twitter, mousey, but bitingly present. He should know the sound. Not a cardinal or a robin, or even a grosbeak. But he knew what it was, having heard the unusual high pitched chirping sound any number of times on this path.

The sound, he knew for sure, was that of a bald eagle.

Why was it here, now, in July? Eagles were winter visitors, following open Mississippi River water with slowly moving fish easy prey in the languid cold water.

He heard it again and stopped. He pulled off the path and surveyed the tranquil water and the line of trees on the opposite shore, defining the edge of the US Arsenal property. But he could see no eagle, nor other birds either.

But then again the chirping drummed into his consciousness. It had to be near, but where was it? He remembered from long ago that the eagles only spoke in groups – when four or five of them commandeered close-together limbs of a tree across the narrow channel.

The bird song slowed, leaving him perplexed. And as he mounted and started pedaling again, the sound diminished, slowly dimming as he moved away. Then he saw it. A bald eagle, flying over the water, neck stretched parallel to the slough, searching.

But Roger Pice didn't stop. It wouldn't be there on time – right now, or in the future - if he stopped and looked. He knew that.

The radio began.

First with a plaintive strain of pure melody.

But then with the percussive slams of deeply amplified drums. Their boom, boom, boom punched a hole in his drifting pedaling. The staccato thumping penetrated and surrounded him. It seemed to be coming from all around him, one boom box supplanted by another.

Accompanying the drumming - seemingly mixed in with the booms - fragments of words pelted him. Now he was traveling through fog banks of sound, pushing strongly as it taxed more and more of his speed, power, and strength. He struggled.

He ramming through sheer humanity – anonymous people, masses of them. And they all were somehow making sound.

Roger was engulfed, but insulated from it. It did not connect rationally or emotionally with him. He battled through it, but he was not of it.

He came upon two walkers by the side of the path, a couple with their arms intertwined. They stuck to each other as if the light sweat from their striding was glue, or love, or lust. A carnival of phonemes engulfed him as he navigated past them. They radiated waves of sheer sexual attraction. Flesh on flesh; skin on skin, drum stick on drum head. Rue captured him. He wanted to stop and stare, but he couldn't. He had to go on, to continue up the path. The parade was waiting.

Now no radio beat, but another rhythmic popping. But this time he saw it - a lazy fishing boat, it's engine put-putting as it crept close to the rough, rock strewn levee edge. The sound aggravated Roger. Too tinny; too miniscule; too echoing of nothingness after the chaos of the parkway. But as he slowly advanced on the motorboat, it became more and more pronounced. Soon it clogged his head forcing him to unconsciously pace himself with its rhythm.

Push down – pop – push down – pop – push down – pop. And louder and louder. More and more insistent. He had to get away from it. Push down harder; push down faster. Hard; fast. Hard, fast.

Incrementally he passed the boat, its passenger intent on the water ahead of him, not glancing to either side. Only the engine remained, hovering in his ear like a hammering woodpecker.

Or was it a real woodpecker? Downed trees, some leaning against each other, congregated here. Good places for downys, flickers, and the like. The boat engine and the bird pecking merged.

But the percussion came to a halt when she went by again. - the woman in the yellow jersey, now pedaling furiously, and heading right at him. She swerved away at point blank. It was the woman from the incident, tearing away from him. Disappearing down the slanted path.

He should turn and follow her, but he forced himself to continue up river. He had to. He was in the parade.

Roger made the zig-zag turn at the power company, looking behind himself at the bridge connecting Sylvan Island to the mainland. He thought of the awful time in the past, but then he pushed it away, and instead what came up was that even longer ago time when he dared reflexes and perceptions when running on the tangled, snaky trails that snarled through the overgrown island like black spaghetti in a rank, green sauce.

But then from the direction of the island he heard a shout, exuberant and piercing. He craned his head and stared back. Nothing. No one. Then he heard it again. It sounded like, "Hey, Roger, turn. Let's go here," but he couldn't be sure. No one was there.

And he knew if he detoured to the island and searched its paths – if he came to the tip of it - he would find no one. The island was empty. He knew.

After the power company dam and railroad bridge the path separated, becoming twin 10-foot wide ribbons of park enhancements – one a walkway, one for bikes.

He approached a large arena/convention center; which now on the morning of the Fourth of July was silent. After hearing so many other, obtrusive but elusive, sounds, he heard nothing here – where usually he heard a virtual cornucopia of voices, music, and other disparate sounds. On the raucous Fourth no sound came forth.

But the center's vast parking lot seemed to Roger to be filled with activity, silent though it was. Many autos, people, and even large trailers filled the space. Two organized groups of people stood in formation. Nevertheless, Roger passed on.

Between the center and an adjacent hotel in an open lawn rambling with foot paths he noticed a bed of mushrooms. They were Shaggy Manes, frothy stems surmounted by barely opened fleshy umbrellas. He had picked them for his mother at one time, collected them in the past from right here. They were delicious in meatloaf. But that was in the fall. Or was it spring?

He stopped again, parked his bike, and walked to the mushroom uprising just to prove to himself that what he was seeing was real. He reached down and touched one and felt it almost transform between his fingers. It became slim and yellow, with petals instead of the bulbous umbrella. Dandelions!

With disgust, he continued his ride, not looking back at the standing flowers. The hotel had a restaurant and an outdoor patio with tables for dining al fresco. It faced a mooring dock for small boats in the slough. It was a very pleasant area, lively now with morning activity and breakfasting in the moderate heat

He slowed down because occasionally people on foot would cross the path, not realizing, or forgetting, that bicycles could be coming through. That was true today, on this holiday. And Roger almost hit a small group of people – two men and three women who were leaving the patio and walking toward the docks. They looked prosperous and vaguely nautical: shorts, white crew-necked sports shirts on the men and similar, but softer, on the women.

As he stopped, Roger half way recognized them. Had he seen them before here, or was it down at Schweibert Park in Rock Island?

But now abruptly he started to speak, to acknowledge his recognition of them. But they just stared at him, and one of the women, a blonde with strands of dark hair, looked beyond him at the boat and said to the others, "Come on, let's get going if we want to make that parade."

They scuttled away, all seeming to look hard at him, but without recognition, leaving Roger stranded and aghast in the midst of these morning breakfasters.

They got into a boat and he started up the path again, a cloud of obscure memories, wonderment, resentment surrounding his progress.

Now he heard it again -the faint sound of the fishing boat. But it felt elusive and illusionary. No bikers shared the path with him; no dog walkers waded around the edge of the trail. From what he could see of the river, no fishing boat progressed. The put-put had vanished – but not its sound.

As he approached a large tower building very close to the point where the slough divided from the major Mississippi River a wind picked up, creating a whistling around him – a high pitched tone, driving away the put-putting, the rat-a-tat.

But up ahead he could see a parade forming. People dressed outlandishly and some spectators already positioning themselves on the sidewalk, anchored securely in their plastic chairs.

He rode to the front of the vague parade lineup, underneath a bridge to Arsenal Island, at the very start of the slough. A slim, attractive woman ran up with a clip board, but ignored him in favor of a trio of Daniel Boone look-alikes. As she gesticulated with them, he caught a glimpse of "bicyclists" on her listing. It was number 43.

So that was it. Number 43. Back he went, looking for other bikes and bikers. Nobody. But he did find entry number 42, a child's wagon sitting unoccupied close to the end of the line of people and assorted "floats" and displays. Obediently, he waited. Why, he did not know.

Now, with the parade about to begin he was the lone biker. And dressed as he was, he was hardly a parade bicyclist, festooned for the Fourth of July.

But something kept him there, even though he knew he could leave, just turn around and go back. Somehow he felt compelled to stay, to do it.

Little girls in baton twirling outfits fussed behind him, their leader – a florid woman dressed like Martha Washington, lining them up .

All at once, Roger heard a tinny band begin playing up ahead, and he knew the parade was starting. Should he ride his bike or walk it? But the units ahead, including a goat cart just in front of the Tom Sawyer lad pulling the wagon started moving and Gerald mounted his bike and started riding very slowly. He could not figure out where the parade was going, but it was slowly moving.

Just then a flurry of activity behind him turned into a complete drum and bugle corps band almost running to get in place behind him. They were fast, forming into ranks precise and disciplined. As he continued, the band began drumming.

They played no pipes, just drummed, beginning with just a staccato lightness of sound. But as the parade – the wagon in front of him, the goat cart ahead of it, and he riding high on his bike moved ahead, the drumming of the band became increasingly louder and louder. The youngsters in the group seemed to be finding their natural fluidity, marching in pace with their drums.

He was pushed along by them – indeed the whole parade that he could see ahead of him was driven by the drumming. Slowly it became incessant. Commanding.

Roger hardly noticed the scattering of spectators along the route. They were a blur of studied quiet, in direct contrast to the boom, boom, boom, of the drums behind him, surrounding him, becoming part of him.

He clenched his handlebars tightly – the billows of booming inundated his slow parade pace, his entire consciousness suffused with the powerful waves of percussion.

The parade veered from the path after it passed under the bridge. It simply disappeared to Roger, where he could not discern.

But Roger didn't follow. He kept on. He kept riding, a flux of booming sound pushing him up the path – up river.

Boom lay, boom lay - boom lay, boom.

And Roger continued riding

Last chapter

Eventually Roger's landlord realized that Roger was not living in his apartment, in fact that the door to his place was unlocked. Big George, the landlord, entered and found the place sparse and neat. A few items of clothing were hanging in the small closet and the cabinet next to the empty refrigerator contained three cans of corned beef hash, one carton of Kraft spaghetti mix, and two small cans of tomato paste. That was about it.

Except the top of the one table in the room held a small sheet of paper with a key folded inside. Written on it was the following:

"Landlord, I had to leave in a hurry. Please, if you could be so kind, take this to the First Security Bank and tell the kind man there, Bill, that I will not be using the safe deposit box anymore. He can empty it. Francis Balch.

Three days later, Big George, on one of his errands to Rock Island's downtown, stopped in the bank and told Bill what he had found in the room and gave him the key. Bill asked George to be a witness when he opened the box. He also asked Janice Hult, a bank teller, to be with them.

All three entered the bank's large vault and Bill proceeded to unlock the safe deposit box.

It was empty of all papers, cash, and antique gold coins.

But it did have a pair of shoes stuffed into it. They were brown Moc-a-Steps.

When Bill took them out, he dropped one of them. When it hit the floor, a scattering of coins rolled across the vault space. A piece of paper was caught between two of them. It said:

"These coins belong to Sylvan Slough. Please give them to the lady who rides her bicycle wearing a yellow shirt. I think her name is Jane. She can use the coins to possibly improve the slough."

Jane and Bill thought long and hard, and about a year later started the Sylvan Slough White Swan Project, whose task became to turn Sylvan Slough into an area-wide cultural, historical, recreational and entertainment venue.

The officers of the association's board consisted of:

Chairman: Jane Fleming
Vice Chairman: Duane Holstrom
Treasurer: Bill Fleming
Media and Graphic Specialist: Bobby Scott

24905758R00110

Made in the USA
San Bernardino, CA
11 October 2015